GAMEBIRD

By

ADRIAN KEEFE

SPARSILE
BOOKS

E Noon

1

It's April. A diminutive green figure sporting a canary yellow backpack is marching along a country road. Low cloud contributes to high humidity, an all-pervasive stickiness. They said there would be showers, some heavy. But it's alright, he's come prepared: an anorak with a hood, over-trousers, walking boots freshly waxed.

An old man comes round the corner with a dog.

'Where you off to then?' the old man asks, shuffling to a halt. 'Looks like you're goin' on an adventure.'

'I am,' he says proudly. 'I went on the number 37 bus and now I'm walking to-'

'Why you dressed like that then?' The old man reaches out, a leathery hand, brushing the green anorak. 'You goin' to solve a mystery? Somethin' like that? You one o' the Famous Five? Is that it? You goin' to 'ave a rip-roarin' time, and when you get home 'ave lashin's o' ginger beer?'

'I don't drink alcohol,' he says, recoiling from staring straw-coloured eyes.

The dog barks.

He pushes on.

'Alright, alright! 'Old yer 'orses. Oi'm jest talkin' to this young adventurer. Hey! Where's 'e gawn?'

'I've got to go now. I've got to keep to my schedule. It's all written down.'

He turns his back on the old man's mutterings and the dog's barks.

The road is sinuous, a dark-green tunnel. The adventurer keeps close to the right-hand side, pressing flat against the hedge when hearing a vehicle. Apart from these occasional times, he's mostly looking down at his Ordnance Survey map in its waterproof pouch dangling from his neck. He worked out a ten-mile circular route, went over it in pencil on the bus. He's looking out for the West Downs Way, which should be coming up on the left with a West Downs Way sign. It's not round the next bend, or the one after that, and maybe he's missed it. The sky darkening, the leaves rustling, the birds agitated; there's nowhere on the road to shelter from a downpour. Maybe the signpost fell down or it's hidden in the foliage. There have been turnings onto locked gates leading to farms; fields, surrounded by antechambers of mud, clay; entrances oozing outwards like river deltas.

Around another bend there is a turning, on the right, neither waymarked, nor guarded or muddied. The sun reveals herself, the flowers turn their heads, wafting perfume in the hope of luring pollinators through the gap. The birds, the leaves, go quiet. Looking up from his map, he takes in banks of colour on either side, strips of young wheat dividing hedgerows rising up to the horizon, funnelling the gaze. Breaching the opening to see properly, the map falling from his fingers, his trajectory altered, a gamebird shot through the heart. Not noticing the gate, prostrate in the shade, stag beetles grappling over conjugal rights, he takes in exultant bugle, cowslips, red clover, unfurling moist petals. He takes in swelling wheat set against slate blue; hedgerows, burnished, bowling across hillsides; puddles transformed into silvered pondlets teeming with life; Lombardy poplars beneath blue hills, twinkling in a heat haze; the track—two slightly paler bands of grass, ghostly remnants of a bygone era, converging into the distance.

Treading cautiously between tussock and tyre track, the dazzling points of colour on either side urging him on. A cool tailwind eases his progress, bending the grasses in the direction of travel, the sun shines over his shoulder, the map swings from left to right in time with staccato steps.

The sun, the breeze, the grass, the hedges, the wheat, keep him company for half a mile while the soft belly of the land conceals the entrance, the hills maintain their distance, the trees close in. By the time the poplars have garlanded him with catkins, the West Downs Way is forgotten. Past the line of trees, meeting the hedgerows on the flattened banks stripped of colour, blanketed with marsh grass, the track snakes to the right, petering out before a boarded-up house ringed with briars. Once white, now the colour of peeled apple, sitting alone and at the bottom of a hollow, the house could be compared to an antlion peeping from its lair, surrounded by bog rather than sand. The land rises up all around, overlooked by the poplars in front, a woodland of beech, birch and oak behind, a majority of hawthorn bushes at the sides.

An overgrown garden backs onto the house. Spotting a bench with a twisted metal back, the diminutive form wades through undergrowth, brushes off dirt with his sleeve, sits down, takes off his backpack, brings out a Tupperware box. Unable to stay put, peanut butter sandwich in hand, he picks up a stick with the other, thrashes at the tangled vegetation, carries out a full inspection. Every window is boarded-up with meticulously-cut sections of planks turned green, the nail heads orange. Not one board has fallen, no gaps between any two, no glass visible, neither are the doors. A big house: three storeys; such are its intricacies, its irregular form, it appears to have grown rather than been built. The storm clouds have blown away, replaced by soft white clumps, amongst which the sun flits between, behind; the house a shimmering jewel.

Counting twenty-two windows, he returns for the other half of his sandwich to accompany a recount. There is one more, he must go round a third time, say the numbers out loud. Tripping over a root, dropping the remaining mouthful, he loses his place, regroups, returns to the challenge with a packet of Monster Munch. Twenty-two again, he must go round once more to be certain.

Nine times he circles, unable to settle on an undisputed number, his lunch-box empty. Checking his watch, he won't be able to complete his pencilled circuit in time, reluctantly deciding to retrace his footsteps to the bus stop, or rather, the one opposite. Consulting a fold-out timetable, the 37s are hourly, he hopes to make the 16.04.

Packing up his things, stretching, a green sapling, he leaves the garden the way he came in, passing by the front of the house. A creak from within. Stopping, listening intently at the door, he hears the grass and the trees whisper.

Rejoining the path, the breeze has picked up, he drops his head towards the grass pointing at the house behind him. Once out of the shade of the poplars, the sun in his face, blinding, hot, still he doesn't undo a single button on his anorak. The sun grows fiercer, he leans into the wind, the grass lies flat, trembling. A strange feeling passes over him when squinting at the gap in the hedge—no more than a black smudge at this distance—climbing towards it as if going up a down escalator. The pinpoints of colour shine too bright to offer any succour, the wheat white hot, a motorbike ripping up the silence.

Received back to the green tunnel by a tractor hauling livestock, he's nearly knocked off his feet. Rumbling by, between the slats, cowering, wide-eyed, skidding on excrement, lambs to the slaughter. The tunnel darkens presently, a few fat raindrops herald a deluge, the road white with splashes, subsiding, to be replaced by persistent rain.

The bus is nineteen minutes late. Unusually, a B7TL, he must remember to log the registration.

'I've been on a walk in the countryside,' he says to the driver, and anyone else who might hear, which is the whole bus.

The driver, who he doesn't recognize, says nothing, doesn't look at the proffered travel pass, promptly sets the vehicle in motion, whereupon, stumbling down the aisle, he's flung onto a seat.

'I've been on a walk in the countryside,' swivelling round, he tells all three passengers on the lower deck, two of whom wear earphones,. None look his way, and four heads jolt in unison as the bus goes over a pheasant.

'I saw a big white house and it had twenty-two or twenty-three…' Trailing off as if still trying to count them, his eyes rest on shining tarmac.

Lost in thought, words occasionally form on his lips, to go no further, as the number 37 heads into a city in full spate. Stopping at the bus station, the driver cuts the engine and all the passengers get off. Save one. He's still thinking about something as the driver presses buttons, counts the money; and even when he's gone outside for a cigarette, returned, started the engine and lets people on, the mouth is making shapes.

Passing through the city centre, the double-decker half-filled, when a girl sits next to him, he pipes up once more.

'I've been on a walk in the countryside and I found a big white house with boarded-up windows.'

'That's nice,' the girl says, taking her phone out of her handbag.

'It had twenty-two or twenty-three windows and I'll need to go back to count them again. They were boarded-up and I couldn't see inside at all.' He makes a tiny hole with forefinger and thumb, holding it up to his eye to clarify the point.

'I see,' she says, scrolling down.

'I wonder who used to live there and why they had so many windows.' He pauses for a moment as an ambulance goes by. 'I wonder why they moved away, if they got bored or died or something, and I wonder why no one lives there anymore?' Inclining his head towards the girl without looking at her, he shakes his finger, continuing in hushed tones. 'I think something happened there, something bad. I think it might have been murder, a very bad murder with lots of blood splattered everywhere.' His eyes are big and he spreads out his hands to show the extent of the splatters. 'That's why no one has lived there for years, and you can tell because of all the bushes, and the weeds growing in the garden and everything.'

Noticing a double seat has become available further down the bus, the girl takes it.

'I think there's a ghost.' Turning back to the window, he draws one in the condensation. 'I heard it roaming up and down the hall. I think it's restless and needs to be let out. If someone had a crowbar they could let it out. I'd do it myself, only I wouldn't be allowed to have a crowbar. I'm going to go back there on my next day off to get to the bottom of it. I'm not afraid of ghosts. Not me, noooo! Not even a tiny bit. Ghosts are just like people, and if you're nice to them, they're nice back. That's what I think anyway.'

When his stop approaches he rings the bell and waits for the bus to pull over in case he falls. Memorizing the registration, he enters it in his logbook, along with the make, number, date, time, before leaving the shelter. It's raining again. But it's alright, he came prepared: an anorak with a hood, over-trousers, walking boots freshly waxed.

2

It's the next day. The adventurer is going to work. He went to bed at 02.14 last night, after watching a DVD, lay there until his watch (synchronized to the nearest atomic clock, accurate to within 0.00001 of a second) changed from 11.59 to 1200 hours, as he always does before his first shift. He's done his housework, he's prepared his food for tonight, he's laid out his uniform. There's nothing left to do except sit in front of the telly with Snowdrop on his lap. He has his tea, gives Snowdrop hers, reads the Going to Work List on the back of the front door out loud twice, checking everything's in order as he goes along. Feeling his keys in his pocket again, he puts on his green anorak, slings the yellow backpack over his shoulders, and, ensuring his keys are still in his pocket a fourth and final time, he paces up and down the narrow hall until the time changes from 17.29 to 17.30 before going out the door.

Marching down the corridor, about to take the door to the stairwell, he notices Mrs Jenkins from 1918 standing beside the lifts.

'Hello Mrs Jenkins.'

'Oh Spencer, it's you. I hoped you were going to work today, and then I could accompany you in the lift.'

'Are you going down to zero Mrs Jenkins?'

'The ground floor, yes.'

'You're not getting off at five again?'

'No Spencer, I only went to the fifth floor once, and that was months ago. I'm going all the way to the bottom. I need milk.'

Hesitating for a moment, he whispers 'milk' a few times as if he's forgotten what it is, before pressing the already lit-up button.

'I'll come down to zero with you Mrs Jenkins.'

They stand there, listening to the workings of the lift far below, the doors opening and closing as people got off on other levels.

'How will you get up again Mrs Jenkins?'

'If that nice West Indian is there, I'll ask him if he'll escort me, otherwise I'll have to wait for Mr Grimes to come back from his shift at the meat factory.'

Presently, the lift arrives, and an elderly man with a red face blunders out in a cloud of stale alcohol and urine.

'Evening ladies,' he says, raising his hat.

'Hello Mr Macready,' Spencer says.

Mrs Jenkins purses her lips as they enter the lift, while Spencer presses the ground floor button, and, lurching from side to side, Mr Macready totters off, his blue plastic bag clinking, as the doors come together.

'I don't think I've ever seen that man without a drink in him, not in all the years I've lived here,' she says. 'How's your mother by the way?'

He looks down. 'Just the same.'

'I'll never forget the time she knocked on my door and asked if I had any drink, said she'd pay me back, and I told her I didn't have any, but she didn't believe me, and pushed past-'

'Well,' he cuts her short, 'you won't ever see me drunk Mrs Jenkins, because I don't drink alcohol at all. Not at all ever, not even my birthday or Christmas.'

'Of course, you're sober as a judge aren't you,' Mrs Jenkins says as the lift stops at the thirteenth floor.

Spencer's heart beats fast, but it's a burka with two small children, to whom she speaks crossly in her language, and the small children, who stare at Spencer, look suitably chastised.

'Yes, that's very true. I've never seen *him* sober and I've never seen *you* drunk!' and she laughs out loud.

She's still laughing when the lift stops at the ninth floor —accelerating Spencer's heartbeat again, but it's a man in a wheelchair—and hasn't completely subsided when she says goodnight and to watch out for dog dirt and syringes, and they leave the building and go their separate ways. He doesn't know why she's laughing or what judges have got to do with it, but knew better than to ask.

As soon as he's alone on the litter-strewn path, he stops and looks all around him, repeating the action every few paces, like a blackbird hopping across a lawn, until he's on the main road where there's plenty of people. Since the first incident, he no longer wears his headphones, at least not when he's near the building, and, to be on the safe side, he doesn't put them on until he's on the train. Robert said it was safe to wear them from then onwards.

Even when on the busy road he looks back towards E

block one final time to make sure no one's following him. No, it's just the block of flats standing there on its own, set apart from the others like an afterthought.

The train is seven minutes late. Disappointingly, it's the same locomotive as always, with the same eight coaches, but still he enters the number in his logbook he carries everywhere—trains at one end, buses at the other.

It's a low-level train, going right across the city and out the other side, unlike the mainline trains, which all terminate at one of two mainline stations. He's been on every railway in the city, of which there are many more low-level lines. He's been on most of the buses as well—and three that no longer run. He'd go on boats and planes more often than he does too, which is hardly at all, if only they fitted into his journeys, because he loves all forms of transport; well, public transport at least, as he's never been on a horse and can't ride a bike. Motorbikes and mopeds are out of the question of course, and also cars (unless someone else is driving) and he can't afford taxis.

He gets out at the end of the line, the terminus, from which it's a ten-minute walk to the motorway service station, where he works, in a supermarket as a shelf-stacker.

Diesel is standing outside, smoking a cigarette before she starts her shift, a nineteen-hundred to seven-hundred-hours like Spencer's.

'Alright Spence. How's it hanging?'

Pausing for a moment, he's about to say something until she interrupts.

'Uh, uh, uh.'

'A little to the left thank you.'

'You need to say it quicker. Don't think about it. Just say, "a little to the left," straight away every time, like that.' She snaps her fingers.

He's about to argue, but knows it's pointless. Months and months it's been going on, and slowly she's winning.

'Evening Spencer,' Ali, the security guard, says.

'Evening Ali.'

'Red Bull's just pulled in,' Ali says to Diesel.

'Alright. I'm not blind.'

They go in, and two of them attend to the delivery.

Soon he gets down to the meat and potatoes of his job, which is stacking shelves, with his 'wagon', as Diesel calls the merchandising trolley, although he helps out with big deliveries as well. It's all hands on deck, seeing as it's just the two of them in the warehouse on nights—or at least *their* nights, because there's Old Bob and Lewis on A night-shift—three on, three off, that's how they work it. She gets the boxes for him and he distributes the stock to the various locations. She has all the information—it comes up on her screen, and she has everything ready for the next load when he returns about an hour later. If there's no more boxes to go out, especially early in the week, he has other chores, like going round the shelves and turning the labels to the front, sweeping, taking rubbish out, stuff like that. He's never idle.

He's had lunch, as they call it, even though it's the middle of the night, it's between two-hundred and three-hundred hours, the checkout assistants' 'dead hour', when they sometimes put their feet up on the conveyor belts. He's in eleven, the savoury snacks aisle, the aisle he's in most often—night workers fill up their baskets with crisps and Red Bull.

'Where's the sandwiches?'

Spencer takes his headphones off and looks up from a box of Walker's multi-packs—trucker-packs they call them.

'What kind of sandwiches, sir?'

'What kind?'

The man's cross-eyed and unsteady on his feet.

'What kind? I'll find them myself. What kind!'

Swivelling, he puts a foot in the box of multi-packs, bursting a few and scattering others as he kicks the box halfway down the aisle. Spencer jumps up.

'Don't worry about that sir.' He knows the things to say to calm down customers; it was part of the training. 'We get the money back on damaged stock. The sandwiches are usually in the fridge beside the kiosk, which is by the main entrance, but at this time of night they'll be discounted, and there could be some freshly made up at the deli counter over here...'

'It's alright, I'll find them myself. I only come in this shithole for a sandwich. I don't need a guided tour.'

'I was only trying to help sir.'

'Why do they even let your kind work here anyway.'

Spencer's about to ask what he means, as it's unclear, but thinks better of it, leaving the man to wander off in the wrong direction for both the kiosk and the deli counter, and returns to salvage what he can of the multi-packs. On the way, he pauses in the produce aisle, finding he's stopped by the leeks, straight, green, like mossy planks of wood.

When he tells Diesel about the customer and asks what he meant by his last remark, she says he should have called security, that's what they get paid for, and leaves it at that. She's playing a game on her phone and he knows better than to bug her. He puts the damaged stock down next to her so she can log it. Without looking up, she opens a packet of cheese 'n' onion, and carries on with her game.

She's sorted out his next load: female hygiene, skin products and 'smellies', as she calls anything perfumed. She's always telling him how she doesn't use any of that gunk, how it's a load of bull, women don't need it, and only has carbolic soap and pills in her bathroom. He doesn't doubt it, only he wonders where she gets this kind of soap, because he knows for a fact they don't stock it. Not that he ever goes in other supermarkets, not when he has a discount card. She doesn't wear make-up either, and has an unusual hairstyle for a lady, what with it being shaved at the sides and long at the back, and she doesn't seem to care that it's grey. Unlike the other women there, she mostly talks to men in her breaks, she doesn't bring a handbag either, and has a big bunch of keys on a chain attached to her belt, which she's forever jangling and spinning. The other thing about her is her badge with 'muff diver' on it, and when he asked what it meant, she told him to look it up in the dictionary, but he couldn't find it.

When he's down the women's aisle, a nurse asks him a question about sanitary products, which of course he doesn't know the first thing about, goes red and giggles.

'Oh, grow up!' she says and walks off.

He follows her, at a distance, and goes to see who's on the tills, but there aren't any women, except Uzma, and he doesn't think she'll know about sanitary products. He's not going to bother Diesel either because she probably thinks they're a load of bull.

Customers ask him a lot of questions, two or three an hour, and it's because there's no one else on the floor on nights. He'd been put on nights so he didn't get in the way of customers, he heard them say that to Anita, the job coach, at the interview.

He likes helping customers if he can. The only problem is sometimes he can't, and they walk away, saying it's alright, they'll ask someone else, or something like that. He loses his place in his audiobook of course, there is that. Tonight he's listening to *Harry Potter and the Deathly Hallows*, so it doesn't matter, because he knows it almost word for word.

Near the end of his shift he bumps into Aggie and Jean, who have just come on, when he's putting out the papers, which is Martin at the kiosk's job, and Diesel's always on at him about not doing other people's jobs, but he doesn't mind. The best part of this job is cutting the plastic tape holding the newspapers together with a Stanley knife, and no one's told him he's not allowed to.

'Alright me old mucker?' Aggie says with her funny accent, while they flick through the women's magazines. 'Have you found the stripy paint yet?'

'I've told you before, we don't stock it, and the only thing I can think of is stripy chocolate spread, which has brown and white-'

'What about dehydrated water?'

'You know we don't have that kind of water. I've told you twenty-seven times.'

'Leave the poor boy alone,' Jean says.

They put the magazines back in the wrong places and go off to start their shifts. It's six. Time to empty the bins and put all the cardboard out the back for Dave G to take away.

As he leaves, Maciek, another security guard, pulls him by the backpack strap and he nearly falls over.

'Where do you think you're going? Did you find out about the whisky delivery?'

'I asked Diesel.'

'I told you to find out yourself.' Maciek prods Spencer hard in the ribs.

'But I didn't know the answer. She asked me why I wanted to know, because I'm not allowed to help with the alcohol deliveries. It's because of insurance. I said it was for a friend.'

'What? You better not have mentioned me you fucking spastyczny.'

'I didn't Maciek, honest I didn't.'

'Alright, fuck off home to Mummy.'

'I don't live with Mum.'

He knows that this isn't right, how Maciek behaves, but sometimes there's nothing you can do and it's only words. He doesn't understand what's so important about the whisky anyway. Even before this business with the whisky Maciek made him feel uncomfortable. Some of his teeth are missing and he has a tattoo of a snake on his neck and ACAB on his knuckles, which Diesel says is bad, but won't say why, and he's afraid to Google it in case he gets into trouble.

He's glad to be on the train again. The first shift's the worst. He can't sleep in case he misses his station, but he can rest his eyes. Stephen Fry's voice is soothing, even though he doesn't need to listen to what he's saying, tuning in and out. Another reason why he hasn't been paying much atten-tion to this audiobook is because of the white house with the boarded-up windows.

He's looking forward to going back there on his next day off, which is Thursday, and today's Tuesday. Tuesday, Wednesday, Thursday. That's three days. How can it be three days when he's already done one shift? He counts them on his fingers. Maybe you don't count Thursday. He could ask that lady, but he better not, not after what happened the last time he asked a stranger a question.

3

It's Thursday, Spencer's on his way back to the white house with the boarded-up windows, and he still doesn't know if it's been two days or three. He wears his headphones on the bus, but not when he's walking on a narrow road without a pavement. Robert told him he needs to keep his wits about him on country roads, and he hopes they are. He's listening to a *Buffy the Vampire Slayer* audiobook. It's called *Inca Mummy Girl*, and he listens to audiobooks three times to get all the facts straight. Stories about vampires are his favourites, although he likes werewolves, zombies and wizards almost as much. He likes some sci-fi too, especially *Star Wars*, *Star Trek* and *Doctor Who*.

Sunnydale melts away when church bells sound out across the farmland, until, that is, in passing a pub, he sees beer barrels rolling down a chute.

Again, the sun comes out when he turns off the road, buffing up the flowers, anointing the wheat, silvering the pondlets and the poplars, the wind shepherds him along, and the grass bows towards the white house with the boarded-up windows.

He's remembered to bring his sketchpad, a Christmas

present from Mum, with a painting of a steam train on the front. It's not accurate though because it doesn't have a steam dome, and it's annoying when artists get things wrong. That's why he prefers photographs. He pointed out the mistake to Mum, but she got cross, said she'd take it back if he didn't stop going on about it.

His twenty-nine Lego trains have many more mistakes, but he doesn't mind that so much because they're small and made of plastic bricks, and he knows they can't get moving parts such as pistons and wheels exactly right. He keeps them in their original boxes in a cupboard, and doesn't build them much anymore, only when a train enthusiast visits him, which isn't very often, or even never. He doesn't bring them out when his sister visits with her children either, not after the time Nathan pulled a headlight off his Hogwarts Express measuring approximately seven-point-five millimetres, held it tightly in his hand, and didn't let go until he was asleep, and Linda found it in the cot the next morning. The thing was, Spencer didn't realize, and spent three hours searching for it under all the furniture, in drawers and cupboards—even emptied out the cat litter. On top of that, Linda wouldn't post it back, said he could wait until the next time she came. All Linda cared about was how Nathan could have swallowed it and had to have his stomach pumped in hospital.

Anyway, he's going to draw the house when he's had his packed lunch; four drawings, one of each side. It's so that he can be certain about the number of windows, and will make sure he draws all of them, even the little ones in the roof. He can show Robert what the house looks like as well, and Robert will be impressed with him because he's going to do a good job, and Robert's always saying he should do more drawing and it's a shame to waste a talent. He does draw sometimes, but mostly vampires and wizards, things like that, and Robert says he should draw from life, like a real artist.

When he starts the first drawing, which is of the front of the house, he finds he has to sit quite far back to see all three floors clearly, and the roof and the chimneys. He finds a rickety chair with flaky paint and mould, and using that makes his task easier because he can rest the sketchpad on his lap.

It's going extremely well, and he can't wait to show Robert. Then he realizes it's too big and he won't be able to get it all in, and has to start again. He's using a pencil with a rubber on the end, except he's drawn the lines too hard to rub out, and he does the second drawing with a lighter touch in case it goes wrong again. He draws the boards and the nails carefully, then wishes he hadn't, because it takes so long, and now he has to keep it up.

By the time he's finished two sides of the house he *really* wishes he hadn't drawn the boards and nails so carefully, because it's already taken an hour, and it will be dark by the time he gets off the bus if he's not careful, and he doesn't like to walk to E block when it's dark, not after the last time. It's too late though, he's got to keep it up. The trouble is he has to look up for each individual line. He had no idea it would take this long, it's a bit boring and he's making more and more mistakes. Then, while he's doing the third drawing, which is of the back of the house, and he's finishing the boards of a small window in the roof, he notices one of the boards is wonky and that's because it's missing a nail, the bottom one. Then, looking across at the other window in the roof, he notices more missing nails, in fact all three boards are without the lower nails on that one, and it looks like they're at an angle and sticking out from the window a bit at the bottom, as if the window is open a bit. Of course, it's possible it was like this before, but it's odd none the less. Maybe it's the ghost, and he's been trying to get out. He imagines the ghost as a lady actually, although that could be because you don't usually see ghosts' feet, and it looks like they're wearing long white dresses.

Just then, he hears the wind whistling in the poplars, and it reminds him he's all alone. He finishes the back and the other side as quickly as possible, while making sure he gets everything right, and now he's looking all around as well as looking up, because it feels spooky, as if there's someone watching him, and he thinks maybe it wasn't such a good idea to have listened to a *Buffy* story before he came here, even though he tries to tell himself vampires aren't real. He's still thinking about the murder, the one that caused the white house to be boarded-up and not lived in for so long. He'd rather not think about either vampires or murders right now, just concentrate on finishing the drawings quickly, and get back on the road. Think about something nice, he says to himself, think about AEC Routemasters and the Flying Scotsman, both of which he's been on.

He's so relieved when he's finished, and can put the sketchpad in the backpack and get away from there.

When searching for the start of the path in the long grass, he notices there seem to be a lot more footsteps than there should be. Not on the actual path, where the grass has been trampled into a long, thin line, but before the path proper, within about twenty metres from the front door, where there's no path at all. This is the second time he's been here, and although he's circled the house many times, he's only walked across this bit three times. Maybe someone else has been here, not a ghost or a vampire or anything; no, a real person. Yes, that'll be what's happened. Someone saw the flowers and walked down to the house —not someone scary or anything—someone just like him, someone nice. Yes, that'll be it. Still, no need to hang around, and he jogs for a bit, until he's past the poplars, whispering away to themselves.

Back on the long, straight section, he's unaware of the view not looking as pretty this way, how the sun's in his eyes, the wind's picked up and pushes him back. He's too distracted checking for ghosts and vampires in front, behind and on the banks, and he knows how fast they can move from all the films and TV series he's watched.

He hurries back for the 17.04, which must have been on time because, out of breath and red in the face, he arrives at the bus stop at 17.07, and has to wait for the 18.04, and now it probably will be getting dark when he's on the path to his block, where most of the lights have been vandalized and aren't working.

The driver on the bus—a Volvo Olympian—is the chatty one with no hair.

'Hello there, Spencer. How are you? Haven't seen you lately. Been on a walk have we? Where to this time?'

But Spencer doesn't feel like talking and says very little. He still feels a bit scared and wants to forget about it, and will sit quietly looking out the window, and not listen to the *Buffy* story. Not that he's rude or anything. He knows to turn the corners of his mouth up and say thank you, things like that.

If only it was a Routemaster, or a Regent even. Then he would be captivated by all the features, and the lovely upholstery of old buses which always smells so nice. These new buses might be roomier, and less rattly, but just don't hold the interest, and his mind keeps wandering back to the white house with the boarded-up windows—*twenty-three* boarded-up windows—because now he knows the total without a shadow of doubt.

He's still thinking about those windows in the roof and something trying to get out, when he's on the path back to E block, and it's dark.

A tracksuit appears in front of him. Turning on his heel, he's about to run, but there's another behind him, and a couple more at the sides. Before he knows what's happening, his arm is being twisted behind his back, they're packed in tight around him and leading him away. He doesn't dare look up, and goes limp from fear and powerlessness. Even though they're all wearing hooded tracksuits and baseball caps, he knows who they are. They take him round the back of the car park, behind a wall, where no one goes, and it's just rubbish and weeds, and smells of wee, and it's extra, extra dark, and his heart feels like a caged animal jumping inside his ribs.

One of them has him in a headlock and he can't move a muscle. Another holds a knife up to his face, and he only knows this when he sees it glint, and then he sees it's got a jagged edge like baby shark's teeth. One of these two, he can't be sure which—it could even be both of them—uses the same body spray as him; Adidas Ice Dive. It comes in a black plastic container with blue lines like scratches on glass. The others stand there in the background, three or four black shapes, and Spencer can see the peaks of their baseball caps darting from side to side.

'Do 'im, do 'im, do 'im!' one in the background says.

He's shaking so much, and the blade's so close, he thinks he might cut himself accidentally.

'Right, you little retard. Listen to what I've got to say, an' listen good,' the one with the knife says.

There's a bit of light on his face, and Spencer remembers him from before, on account of his freckles and being so frightening.

'We know you went to the rozzers, so don't deny it. They come lookin' for us, but they ain't got nuffin' on us. My dad did time, an' it fucked 'im up so bad he 'anged 'imself. Well I'll tell you summink. I ain't never doin' time for no geezer, let alone a fuckin' mong. So you keep this shut. Speak to anyone about us again an' I'll fuck you up.'

His face is so close, and he's so angry, that he's spitting on Spencer when he says these things, and his face is scrunched up like a scrunched-up ball of paper. Spencer feels metal touch his lip and emits a tiny squeal.

'Do I make myself clear?'

The knife presses into his top lip and it could go in.

'I said, do I make myself fuckin' clear?'

Spencer is trying to say he understands, but the words are stuck in his throat, and he can't even nod because of the headlock. The Adidas Ice Dive is confusing him and his heart is about to explode out of his chest wall like the creature in the first Alien film, made in 1979.

'This is your last chance. I'll cut you from 'ere to 'ere.'

He traces a line from the corner of Spencer's mouth to his ear with the tip of the blade. 'Will you keep this shut?'

'Do 'im, do 'im, do 'im!' the one in the background says.

'Yes, yes, yes! I understand. I won't tell anyone about you.'

Spencer's head is released, the tracksuits melt away, and sliding down the wall, he's sick down his green anorak.

He waits there in case he's sick again, and his heart's thumping, his head's spinning, and he can smell sick mixed with wee.

He waits and he waits.

Later, he's on the bed. After a few attempts at getting *in* the bed, he gave up. It feels safer on top. He's holding his knees and rocking back and forth, something he used to do when he lived with Mum, and he's reciting statistics about the Flying Scotsman, such as length, weight, number of wheels. He made his tea earlier, and put it on the plate, and watched the steam coming off it. The cutlery reminded him of the knife, even though all his cutlery's plastic. He fed Snowdrop of course. He did that straight away. Quite a bit of her food ended up on the floor, but she ate it just the same. He tried to have a bath, because he thought that might be a good idea, and filled the bath and put the bubble bath in. He undressed and was about to get in, had one foot poised over the steaming water. Then he pulled it back again, put his dressing gown on and took the plug out. He's seen too many films where people are pulled underwater, and they don't come back up, and the water goes red.

So, he'll just sit like this for a bit, or even all night.

Snowdrop's sitting on the bed as well, at the other end from Spencer, and her eyes are wide open. There's no escape, there's nothing either of them can do, they'll just have to sit it out. The only good thing about the situation is Spencer's not thinking about ghosts or vampires anymore.

4

It's the next day and Spencer's having a bath. Every now and then he remembers the incident from last night, his heart beats faster, and it feels like it's happening all over again. After he's dried himself, he doesn't use Adidas Ice Dive, he throws it in the bin, and he takes the two full containers from the bathroom cabinet, and throws them away as well, and empties the bin in the rubbish chute in the lobby, and waits to hear it land in the skip nineteen floors below before closing the hatch, to make sure it's gone. When he's back in 1919, he thinks about the containers of Adidas Ice Dive some more. He can't stop thinking about them, and wishes he'd taken them to another bin far away. Then he gives Snowdrop her breakfast, and hearing her purring calms him down a bit. Then he has his Rice Krispies, and the snaps, crackles and pops calm him down more.

Spencer has a meeting with Robert today. Robert comes to 1919 once a month, on different days because of Spencer's shifts, but always the same time, fifteen-hundred hours, because Spencer doesn't like change. Before Robert leaves they always write down the date of the next meeting in their diaries, depending on when they're both available. Spencer feels anxious on these days, and the anxiety increases the closer it gets to fifteen-hundred hours. The worst part is the waiting, and he doesn't like to go out anywhere, in case something goes wrong and he isn't back in time. Today he's *very* anxious, much more than usual. He knows it's because of the incident, and although he tries not to think about it, he can't *stop* thinking about it, and he's worried what Robert will say about it, and if anything will happen as a result of what he says. If Robert says he's going to do something about it, anything at all, speak to someone, anything, he's going to get even more anxious; a lot more.

He knows to keep busy, because Robert told him that's the best way to stop worrying about things. The trouble is, he's done all his housework, he's prepared everything for tonight, and there's nothing left to do. He's tried to watch an episode of Stranger Things, because he's only watched it twice so far, but he can't concentrate, and it's too scary, and adds to his anxiety. He listens to *Harry Potter* again on his headphones, and although he can't pay attention to that either, it calms him down a bit, especially when he turns the volume up to seven.

Sometimes he looks out the windows, just to pass the time. It's an amazing view from the nineteenth floor, and he's got binoculars for looking at buses and trains in the distance. Today the view isn't so good because it's overcast, and not just that, it's oppressive, even inside his ears, and looking outside makes him feel worse.

Then he remembers the drawings of the white house with the boarded-up windows in his sketchpad, and looks at them. This calms him down considerably, in fact it feels like a wave of calmness has flowed over him, the pressure in his ears reduces, and the sky lightens. He decides to copy all four drawings out again, only this time he draws them much neater, and uses a ruler, and lies down on the carpet, and Snowdrop sits on his back and purrs loudly, and this makes him almost completely calm, as if the incident happened a long time ago.

When he sees it's 14.42, he panics again, because Robert will be here soon. He tidies up, combs his hair and takes up his position for when a visitor is due to arrive, which is by the living room window, from where he can see the roof of the car park, far below. It's easy to see Robert's car approaching, on account of it being a mustard one-litre, three-cylinder Fiat five-hundred, and different to all the regular cars entering and exiting the car park. Robert says it's yellow, but it's not, Fiat don't do yellow five-hundreds, only mustard ones, it says so in the brochure. Spencer knows a lot about cars, even though he doesn't have one and isn't allowed to drive. It's just one of the things he knows about; he only needs to see a new car a couple of times to be able to spot it from a distance, and remember its specifications, such as brake horsepower, miles to the gallon, cost, colours, acceleration and features that come as standard. It's the same with trains and buses, he doesn't have to try. He reads books about cars as well of course, and watches programmes on telly, and looks at them on the internet, and buys magazines about them.

Not many people in E block have cars, but the ones who do—who are mostly men—usually have big black or silver cars with tinted windows, and they're mostly BMWs, Audis and Mercedes-Benz. They often have rap music playing, and Spencer doesn't understand how they never go anywhere and burn petrol standing still, when these are high-performance cars; the BMW M eight for instance, can generate eight-hundred-and-twenty-three horsepower. Once he saw a black BMW M eight and stopped to inspect it because he'd never seen one before. One of the windows opened smoothly and silently while he was looking at the wheels, and he could make out a man with rings on every finger and sunglasses even though it was dark. Spencer waved to him, and the man waved back with one finger, and perhaps his other fingers didn't work properly. The cars don't look big from up here. From up here they're Matchbox cars, and the rap music a vibration.

Robert knows Spencer likes him to arrive on time, and Spencer usually sees his mustard Fiat five-hundred come round the corner between 14.49 and 14.55. If he arrives later than that, by the time he's standing on Spencer's doormat he will be late, and it could be 15.01, 15.02, and once it was 15.04. Spencer doesn't like Robert to cancel either, even if he's ill. He likes things to go according to plan. Spencer used to have another social worker, Julie, and Julie was very nice, and she was the one who helped him get out of Sunrise and into independent living. She helped him with independent travel as well, and took him on a Routemaster. The only problem with Julie was that she wasn't so good at timekeeping. In the end, because he got so worked up about her being late, and sometimes cancelling, it was decided there should be a change of personnel, and that was when Robert became his social worker.

When he hears the intercom he nearly jumps out of his skin, even though he saw the mustard Fiat five-hundred drive into the car park, and Robert walk towards the building.

Spencer says, 'Hello?' and waits for him to say his name because he's told Spencer fourteen times he must make sure it's the right person before pressing the buzzer.

The first five minutes of the meetings are always the same. They talk about what Robert calls pleasantries and small talk. The first thing he usually says is that Spencer should take his tracksuit top off because it's like a furnace in here, and he should open the window. Spencer does what he's told, but when Robert leaves, he puts his top back on and closes the window. Then Spencer has to ask if he wants a cup of tea, and he says yes, and Spencer makes him one. One time Spencer put the kettle on when he saw the mustard Fiat five-hundred arriving, and by the time Robert came in, the tea was ready, but Robert said that was inappropriate behaviour, and he has to ask him if he wants tea when he arrives. He brings a plate of biscuits with the tea, even though neither of them touch them, because this is what Robert calls a protocol. After he's gone, Spencer puts the protocol biscuits back in the tin, where they will stay until the next meeting. When they got to know each other, and had their first few meetings, straight away Spencer would talk about something he'd done or a film he'd watched, even before he said hello. Now they start off by discussing the weather, and asking each other how they are, to which they both reply 'fine'. Then Spencer has to ask if it's OK to tell Robert his news. If it is OK, he takes his paperwork out, and fills it in while Spencer's talking, because that makes his job easier.

Today, however, Spencer doesn't want to talk about anything and waits to see what will happen.

'What's your address Spencer?'

Robert always asks Spencer what his address is, because he has to put it on the top of the form, along with his contact number, the date and time.

'What's your date of birth again?'

He always asks this too, as well as what his middle name is, and if his emergency contact details have changed.

Today, when Robert's finished all these protocols, he takes another sip of tea, adjusts his glasses, and regards Spencer. There is a pause. Spencer can feel Robert regarding him. It makes his face hot. He watches Snowdrop cleaning herself on her chair.

'Aren't you going to tell me something Spencer? A walk you've been on, a DVD you've seen, or an audiobook you've listened to?'

Spencer concentrates on Snowdrop cleaning herself.

'Surely you've got something to tell me.'

Spencer concentrates hard.

Robert takes another sip, and now *he's* concentrating on Snowdrop; the two of them are concentrating on Snowdrop cleaning herself.

Snowdrop can feel them concentrating on her, it makes *her* face hot, she jumps down, and goes out the room.

As if she's still there, Spencer concentrates on the chair.

'Do you know what I think?'

Spencer is silent.

'I think you have got something to tell me. It's not about a walk, or a DVD, or an audiobook. I think it's something important. Now, would you like to tell me what it is?'

Spencer tries to find something else to concentrate on, but there's nothing, and he sees freckles dancing on the carpet, and his heart picks up the beat.

'I know what it is Spencer; I can see it written all over your face. But rather than forcing you to talk, or putting words in your mouth, I'd rather you told me about it in your own words. Now, I'm going to go to the toilet, and when I come back I want you to tell me all about it. OK?'

The freckles are still there. He's rooted to the spot, and the only thing he can think about is jumping out the window. But who would look after Snowdrop, who's been with him two years, three months and twenty-seven days?

Snowdrop was born in 209, but when the man who lived there died she went upstairs to a family, the Wongs, in 1818, until they moved away, and then Spencer was asked if he'd like to take her, and she came upstairs to him, and he's looked after her ever since. There's nowhere left for her to go up to because Spencer's on the top floor, and next time she goes upstairs, it will be when she goes to Heaven.

Hearing the toilet flush, his heart turns into the caged animal again.

'Well then,' Robert says when he's sat back down and finished the tea in one gulp, 'I'm all ears.'

Spencer wants to check, but his eyes won't go there, preferring to remain with the freckles, or whatever the dots are.

'Alright then,' Robert says with a sigh, 'I'll make it easy for you. It's those teenage boys isn't it? They've been teasing you again haven't they? Well, I'll just have to speak to Mrs Adeoye, the Police Community Liaison Officer, won't I?'

The caged animal makes a bid for freedom.

'Well, what do you expect me to do Spencer? I can't just brush it under the carpet can I? What did they do to you last time? They pulled your backpack off and kicked it about like a football didn't they? And then they threw it in the rubbish skip. Now, if there's no report about this second incident, and you're not going to talk to me about it, you won't talk to Mrs Adeoye will you? Take it easy Spencer, she's on your side, I wish you would understand that. Of course she'll say we need CCTV footage, because otherwise there's no evidence, and of course we'll find out none of the cameras are working, but we have to go through the steps, because that's my job, and that's the procedures.'

Spencer looks at his watch. 15.27. He wishes it was half an hour later, and Robert had to go to his next meeting. At least he doesn't know about the other incidents. He thinks this is the second one, but it's not, it's the eighth, and the next one will be the ninth. He didn't tell Robert about the first six incidents, and he didn't find out about them. He only found out about the seventh incident because Mr Fisher, one of the janitors, saw them throw a backpack in the skip, looked inside it, saw Spencer's name on the cover of his bus and trainspotting logbook, filed a report, and notified Robert.

'I've got to write something Spencer. I know you're not going to tell me, so I'll just put down that they were teasing you again shall I?'

The caged animal's relentless head-butting of his ribs diverts all Spencer's attention. He knows he mustn't tell Robert about the animal, let alone anything else. He feels that if he so much as nods his head, the one with the freckles will find out, and he'll be dragged to the place behind the car park that smells of wee, and stabbed, and bleed to death, and Snowdrop will starve to death.

'That's what I'll write. Then, later, after my next meeting, I'll speak to Mrs Adeoye about—I have to Spencer, that's my job. Spencer, don't worry, we'll get to the bottom of this, and everything's going to be alright.'

Later—after Robert's gone downstairs to see Jackie in 1208 (which is where his next meeting is) although he never says it like that, and will only say he's going to his next meeting—Spencer does the drawings again because he wasn't happy with the last ones. This time he goes over them in pen and fills them in with colour pencils, or at least the boards, which are green, and the roof, which is dark red, but he doesn't have dark red so he has to use red with brown over the top. He feels good after this and sticks the drawings on the wall with Blu Tack so he can look at them side by side. He finds that looking at them calms him down, and when he's made his tea, he looks at them while he eats and doesn't even put the telly on. He had shown the first and second drawings to Robert, but he hadn't looked at them, and said Spencer shouldn't go nosing about derelict buildings that haven't had a risk assessment carried out on them, especially not without authorization, a safety helmet and hi-vis vest. He thought about Julie, his previous social worker, who always liked to see his drawings and once she framed one.

Then he remembers Robert saying he saw something written on his face. So, he goes into the bedroom and looks in the mirror while thinking about the incident, which gives him pains, and the animal starts prowling, and then jumping, and then rattling its cage, and still he thinks about it. He thinks about the one with the freckles, the knife pressing into his lip, the smell of Adidas Ice Dive, the black shapes in the background, the peaks of the caps darting from side to side. He thinks about all of this as hard as he can, and it feels nearly as bad as when it happened, and it really will be like that scene out of the first Alien film, made in 1979, and rather than being stabbed to death, he'll be killed by his heart bursting out of his chest, and Snowdrop will starve to death, and because he doesn't answer when Robert buzzes him for his next meeting, the police will break down the door and discover their corpses. He keeps thinking about all these things, and still he can't see any words on his face, not even one letter. So he goes back to look at the drawings and they calm him down, and then Snowdrop sits on his lap, and stroking her while she purrs loudly calms him down some more, and everything's OK again.

Later, when Spencer goes to bed, he hardly feels scared at all, and neither does Snowdrop, and he sleeps under the duvet, and she sleeps on top.

5

It's the next day, Spencer's last day off before he goes back to work. He's thinking about Robert speaking to Mrs Adeoye, he's thinking about Mrs Adeoye speaking to the teenagers, he's thinking about what the one with the freckles will do to him as a result. One leads to another, there's no way out. Doing the drawings last night made him feel a bit better, but now he realizes they're just drawings, it's not like they're magic or something. The drawings can't stop Robert speaking to Mrs Adeoye, and neither can they stop Mrs Adeoye speaking to the teenagers. He can look at the drawings all he likes, he still has to go out into the real world, and sooner or later, the one with the freckles will get him.

It would be alright if he could stay in 1919 for the rest of his life, except then he couldn't work, and if he couldn't work he wouldn't get any money, and if he couldn't get any money he wouldn't be able to buy any food, and soon after he ran out of food, both he and Snowdrop would die of starvation. The only other option is to jump out the window. Snowdrop would still die of starvation, and he would die as well, except in his case it would be on account of all his bones smashing to pieces, which is what happened to Mr

Sulieman when he jumped off the roof after his asylum was refused.

It's 10.24 and Spencer has to find something to occupy him for the rest of the day—and half the night—because he needs to stay up late the night before his first shift. He could see Derek in 1616. Derek likes trains, and has a Hornby set made in 1957. Derek is always at home on account of being in a wheelchair and not being able to move, and carers come in to feed him, and nurses come in to give him medication and change his dressings. The only trouble with Derek is he asks Spencer to attend to his urges, and no matter how many times Spencer says no thank you—and once said it seventeen times—Derek keeps asking, and eventually he gives in. Derek says the carers and nurses won't do it, even though he said he'd supply them with disposable gloves, and the NHS won't pay for prostitutes. Once Spencer's done it they get back to the trains, and Derek has a lot of trains, and a lot of stories from when he was a boy and all trains were steam trains, not just on heritage railways like they are nowadays.

He doesn't feel like seeing Derek today though, and he doesn't want to go to the day centre either because there isn't usually anyone there who shares his interests. Most of the people who go there are old, and the only conversation Spencer has with them are pleasantries and small talk about illness and death, which he doesn't mind for a few minutes, but not hours on end.

He could see Jackie in 1208, or Walter in 320, both of whom he knew at Sunrise, and they're independent living like him. But Robert says he can't knock on their doors, because their addresses are confidential. It would be alright if he bumped into them, in the lift or somewhere like that, and they invited him in for coffee, and then it would be a social engagement, but otherwise knocking on their doors is strictly forbidden. He doesn't particularly want to be invited for coffee by either of them though, that's the thing, not only because he doesn't like coffee, but because Jackie would just talk about her dolls and Walter doesn't talk at all.

What he feels like doing is going back to the white house with the boarded-up windows, even though Robert told him not to. He looks at the drawings on the wall, stares long and hard at them. If only it was possible to live there. It would be so much nicer to live in a house on its own like that, rather than a tower block with noisy neighbours, having to go up and down nineteen floors every day, and worrying about people like the one with the freckles. It doesn't seem right that no one lives there. It's a big house going to wrack and ruin. Robert wouldn't let him live there though, not even if he wore a safety helmet all the time.

Robert told him not to go back there, said that on no account was he to nose about derelict buildings without authorization. He hasn't nosed about though, and neither his nose, nor any part of him have touched the building. He just likes going there, and looking at it, that's all. You don't need authorization to look at things, and nothing is going to fall down from being looked at.

Now that he's made his mind up, he feels much better about everything. As he spreads peanut butter on his sandwiches, he feels a new lease of life, and is glad to have found something to do.

He closes the door quietly in case Mrs Jenkins comes out, and wants him to go down in the lift with her. This has happened six times, and he finds it difficult to say no to an old lady who's had troubles of her own with other residents.

Apart from the times he's bumped into his next-door-neighbour, he hasn't used the lift since the first incident on December tenth. He doesn't think the teenagers would do anything if he was with Mrs Jenkins, but, by avoiding the lift as much as possible, he reduces the risk. He doesn't know which floors they live on, that's the only problem. If he knew for a fact they all lived on higher floors, or really any floor above the second, he wouldn't worry nearly so much, because the only people he's bumped into on the stairs above the second floor are cleaners or Mr Higgins, the keep-fit fanatic, who says, 'Not bad for a seventy-eight-year-old,' every time Spencer passes him running up and down the stairs.

Even though he's ninety-nine-point-nine per cent recurring certain he won't see anyone before the third floor, he still tiptoes down the stairs right from the start, to be on the safe side, and he's not wearing his heavy walking boots, as he doesn't need them for this walk.

The further he descends, the slower and softer his footsteps become. With each floor he thinks he can't be any quieter, but then finds that, yes, he can, and perhaps he'll be walking on air by the time he's outside. Sometimes he hears a muffled bang or thud, and it's hard to tell where it's coming from on account of the echoes. These sounds, on top of his gradual descent, increase his trepidation, and it feels like the animal will not only burst out of his chest, but out of his ears at the same time, as if it's not just in his chest, it's in his head. This is partly because he's listening so hard his ears hurt, and he's ready to bolt, either up or down the stairs if he sees a cleaner, Mr Higgins, anyone. He has a rest on the twelfth floor, and looking at one of the drawings—which he brought with him—gives him the courage to continue. He looks at another on the eighth floor, and a third on the fourth.

Leaving the fourth floor, below which there's a nought-point-nought per cent recurring with a one at the end chance that someone would use the stairs rather than the lift, he can't stand it any longer, runs as fast as his legs will carry him, two stairs at a time, practically tumbles head over heels down the last flight, hits the door running, his momentum carrying him through, and down the path, where it feels as if he's still plummeting down the stairs, and the paving slabs are in the way, and he doesn't come to a halt until he's on the main road. His eardrums are bursting, and he's panting so hard he has to bend over and take ten deep breaths.

Later, when he's on the bus, and his eardrums and his breathing are normal again, he smiles at his reflection in the window. After all, he's allowed to travel independently, he has a certificate with him to prove it, signed by Julie, and it's up to him where he wants to go, and even though he doesn't have authorization, a safety helmet, or a high-vis vest, he's going to the white house with boarded-up windows anyway.

During the walk from the bus, which is approximately three miles, the first part along a disused railway (where steam trains travelled before the Beeching cuts) the second part along a yellow road on his Ordnance Survey map, he smiles some more. When he thinks about Robert's wagging finger, risk assessments and inappropriate behaviour, none of it matters, and neither does the one with the freckles, who now seems a bit silly.

Today, the sun is half-out, has been all morning; wrapped

in gossamer, a silver disk, bestowing silvery light, watery brightness, indistinct forms, shadows, soft edges, twinkles. The sun can't be expected to come out at the drop of a hat, especially when its appearance goes unnoticed, and sometimes it might already be there, or not appear at all.

Even the house has a sparkle, the green parts faintly luminous like the glow-in-the-dark stars on Spencer's bedroom ceiling. Everything is the same about the house, and he likes that aspect of it, how it's in this secluded place that never changes, except with the seasons. He's not going to inspect or draw it today. He's not going to do anything with it. He just wants to be here that's all. He's going to have his lunch on the bench in the garden just like before, and might go on sitting there if the mood takes him.

As long as he leaves in plenty of time for the 17.04, that way he'll be back before it gets dark, and then there won't be another incident. He'd rather not think about things like that though, not here, not when he's having a nice time to himself, doesn't want to spoil it. He can have those sort of thoughts when he's in E block—and he can't stop them anyway—but not here, not in this special place. The one with the freckles, and people like that, belong in tower blocks, behind car parks, and places like that. They wouldn't come here, because they wouldn't see the point of flowers, trees, boarded-up houses, and things you get in the countryside. So there's really no need to think about those people here, let alone worry about them. Spencer lives in a tower block too, but feels different, is allowed to come here, with or without authorization, or even that he does have authorization, his own special authorization.

He's having his pickled onion Monster Munch, and

he's looking at the trees in the woods with their yellow and white blossom like frozen fireworks, when he hears 'crump' behind him. Looking over his shoulder, his eye is drawn to a window on the ground floor with a black stripe where a board should be. It reminds him of Maciek's teeth, although he'd rather not think about people from work, and can't imagine them in the countryside either. The missing plank is lying in the weeds, and it must have just fallen down, and that's what went crump. It's not even windy, so why it should fall down is a mystery.

Jumping up to take a closer look, Monster Munch in hand, Spencer peers into the sliver of glass exposed by the fallen board. It's dark in there and he can't see anything. When he puts his face up to the gap, cheeks hard against the boards on either side, a smile appears on his face again, because now he *is* nosing about a derelict building. Putting his hands either side of his face to block out as much light as possible he can just about make out shapes within. The more he becomes accustomed to the darkness, and when he's finished crunching the piece of Monster Munch in his mouth and swallowed it, he can see more and more. It's as if it's black and white in there, or rather black and different shades of very dark grey. It's the living room because he can make out a sofa, an armchair, and what looks like a grand-father clock in the corner, a black shape looming over the proceedings. The rug has a pattern and the more he looks at it, the more he can focus on it, and it has funny little shapes, and it looks very old, the kind of rug a wizard might have. There's other things in there, and it looks cluttered and messy, and staring as hard as he can some parts of the room won't sharpen, and seem to be hidden behind cobwebs. At the same time, it looks cosy with its wonky bookshelves, its old wooden things, the kind of things that are nice to touch, or just look at.

He's still smiling when he packs his things up, slings his backpack over his shoulder, smiling when he walks under the line of poplars, smiling as he toils up the track, into a buffeting breeze, while the flowers shake their heads.

He still looks pleased with himself when he's on the bus, but he doesn't talk to anyone about the house. He wants to keep it to himself, his secret place, just for him.

Climbing the stairs of the tower block, running up the first three floors, and slowly from then onwards, he thinks some more about the room he peered into. He can still see it. On one side there was the grandfather clock, then there was the sofa, side-on, then the armchair, facing him. The armchair had something on it, something he couldn't make out in the gloom. He thought it was a pile of clothes; then, as if by magic, the pile tidied into neatly stacked suits on clothes hangers, as if the person who had moved out had been in a rush and left them by mistake.

In hindsight, as he steals up the stairs, it's as if the cobwebs weren't in the room at all, but in his mind all along, and his mind has swept them away, and as well as the torso, the arms and legs of the pile of suits, he can see hands, feet and a head poking out. There was someone sitting in the armchair, and they were looking at him as he was looking at them. The further he climbs, the more the cobwebs dissolve, and the clearer the person becomes. He can see it's not trousers after all; it's a dress, there's a girl with long hair sitting there, and she might even be alive.

6

It's the next day and Spencer's at work. He's very excited today due to the fact that he finally got his Lego model seventy-one-forty, an X-wing Fighter, back from Norman Beazley, who borrowed it three years and one-hundred-and-forty-six days ago. He's brought it in to show Diesel, because she's a Trekkie, she knows how to say a few Klingon phrases, such as, 'your mother has a smooth forehead', and she likes *Star Wars* as well. She always arrives before him, and he can barely contain himself as he goes into the warehouse.

But she's not there, and he has to wait.

It's 19.16 and she still hasn't come in, and he's been outside three times to see if she's smoking a cigarette, and he's asked every member of staff in the building, which is eleven, and no one knows where she is. There's no way of finding out either, and the office is shut. Not only is Spencer crestfallen, he doesn't know what to do, because there's no replacement supervisor, no other staff work in the warehouse, and he's not permitted to use the computer, which has all the information about what stock to put on the shelves, because the Union said it's outwith his jurisdiction.

It's 19.31, and having nothing else to do, he takes the Lego set out of its box and starts building the X-wing Fighter, and having built it so many times before he doesn't need to refer to the instructions. It only takes seven minutes, and almost exactly as he finishes, a man walks in he doesn't recognize.

'Excuse me sir, customers aren't permitted in here,' Spencer says.

'I work in the warehouse at the superstore,' the man says. 'I've just come from there to fill in for your man. That's my chair I think you'll find.'

'Oh, right.' Spencer vacates it and stands there, shifting from foot to foot, while the man sits down. Spencer tries to think of something to say. 'What's your name please and thank you?'

'My name? My name is... Bill...' and he looks down at the ground, 'Poster. Bill Poster. What's *your* name?'

'Spencer Frederick Morton.'

'Spencer, yes,' unfolding his newspaper, he starts to read it, 'I've heard about you. Haven't you got something to be getting on with?'

'Yes, but I don't know how to use the computer. Diesel does it all. She finds out what stock we need on the shelves, locates it for me, and I put it in the merchandising trolley.'

'Is that right? Let's have a look.' Bill folds up his newspaper neatly and turns the computer on. 'Is this yours?' He holds up the spaceship.

'Yes, it's Lego model seventy-one-forty, an X-wing Fighter. It's very rare, especially in good condition, with the box and instructions. I've had it since 1999, which is when it came out, and I was eight years old.'

'Have you indeed? That's interesting. How much is it worth?'

'I don't know, but it's not for sale anyway, because I'm an enthusiast, and I've got seventeen Lego *Star Wars* models, twenty-nine Lego train models and three Lego bus models.'

'Have you indeed? That's interesting. Do you have any other rare ones?'

'Not really. I should say the seventy-one-forty is the rarest. It's exceedingly rare in fact, especially in good condition and—'

'In the box, yes, you said. Seventy-one-forty you say? Let me make a note of that.'

'Are you a Lego *Star Wars* model enthusiast as well?' Spencer's face lights up.

'Well... Yes, yes I am actually. But I haven't got a seventy-one-forty. I've got most of the others, but not this one.'

'What have you got?' Spencer can't believe his luck at meeting a fellow enthusiast.

'What have I got? What *haven't* I got you mean—well, apart from the seventy-one-forty obviously.'

'Have you got a Millennium Falcon?'

'A Falcon? Have I got a Falcon? I've got six. All in mint condition and still in the boxes.'

'Wow!' Spencer's never heard the like.

'But look here.' Bill turns to the computer. 'I can't get it to work. See?' He's pressing keys and nothing's happening.

'Can't you log-on?'

'Not on this computer, no; it won't let me.'

'So, what are we going to do?'

'What are we going to do?... Let me have a think.' He strokes his chin and his eyes revolve. At length, he stops stroking his chin, his eyes stop revolving and he raises his eyebrows. 'I give up.' He puts his feet up on the desk and unfolds the newspaper again.

'We'll need to go up and down all the aisles with a notebook and an HB pencil, and write down all the things we're short of, then find them all, put them on the merchandising trolley and take them to the relevant shelves.'

'The relevant shelves… Yes, I suppose you're right.' Bill doesn't look up. 'I tell you what, you make a start and I'll join you later, when I've finished reading my paper. How does that sound?'

'That sounds good.'

Spencer gets to work. He knows which products run out quickest, and heads straight for the fridge with the cold drinks, followed by the snacks aisle, the bread aisle and the milk section. He needn't worry about produce, day shift do that. He makes a note of all the lines that have run out or nearly run out.

When he goes back through the swing doors to show Bill his list, pleased as punch to be working with a fellow enthusiast, Bill isn't there, so he starts looking for all the items he needs until Bill comes back. By the time he's filled the trolley, Bill still hasn't returned, and he has to put it all on the shelves himself. While he's doing this, customers keep coming up to him, asking for things which the supermarket's run out of and he hasn't got round to filling up. Sometimes they're in his trolley waiting to go out, but other times he has to make a special trip to the warehouse, because he likes to help customers when he can. This slows him down considerably, and as soon as he fills up one aisle, another's half-empty.

'Your job's like painting the Forth Bridge isn't it?' Gloria says, deliberating over the low-calorie crisps, when Spencer's opening a box of Walker's multi-packs.

Spencer nods and turns his mouth up at the corners, which is what he does when people he doesn't know that well say strange things.

Every time he goes back to the warehouse, Bill is either reading his newspaper or not there.

'Nearly finished,' he says, when he is there.

Later, Spencer's putting Red Bull in the fridge for the third time, which he isn't supposed to do, because he's not permitted to handle caffeinated and alcoholic beverages, but customers keep asking for them, saying they only came in for a Red Bull, and what kind of supermarket is this? He doesn't think Bill will ever finish his newspaper, and perhaps he's a slow reader. The fridge is near the entrance, and he sees Bill outside having a cigarette, and he's talking to Maciek.

Just then he puts his head through the automatic doors, and motions Spencer over.

'When did you say that Lego spaceship was made?'

'The seventy-one-forty?'

'Yes, the seventy-one-forty.'

'1999, when I was eight years-'

The doors close.

Returning to the cans of Red Bull, which keep running out, he notices Bill and Maciek looking at Maciek's phone, and after a few minutes they're excited about something. Maybe Maciek likes *Star Wars* Lego as well as whisky. Yes, that's probably it; he's a whisky enthusiast. There's a particular type of whisky the supermarket stocks, and they've run out, and that's why he's so keen to know about the delivery, because he needs that one for his collection. Spencer doesn't know anything about whisky, and he doesn't drink alcohol.

Spencer works through lunch because there's so much stock to go out, and he can't get ahead of himself. It's such a busy supermarket, even through the night, because it's at the motorway service station, and it's mostly lorry drivers, van drivers and shift workers who come in at night, and that's why they need staff to stack the shelves twenty-four hours a day. It wouldn't be so bad if it wasn't for all the customers asking for things, and Spencer can't say no to them.

'I'd help you, but you're so good at your job, and I'd only slow you down,' Bill says when he's in the warehouse.

Increasingly, as the night wears on, Bill's not there—and later he takes a nap with his feet up on the desk and the newspaper over him like a sheet. Must be tired, thinks Spencer, tiptoeing around him. One time, when Spencer goes in there and Bill's sleeping, he pretends it's not really Bill at all, and if he pulled the newspaper away it would be the girl with long hair.

Bill wakes up when Spencer puts out the newspapers and magazines, and helps himself to a Daily Mail.

'Oh no,' he says, 'another one to read. It's never-ending.'

Spencer's getting agitated because he's so behind with everything, and he's got to help with a bread delivery, and take all the rubbish out. He's worried what Les will say when he comes in. Les is the Warehouse Manager and he works nine-hundred to seventeen-hundred hours weekdays, like all Management. Because their hours don't overlap, Spencer has never seen Les, but he hears about him from Diesel, and she says he's never satisfied with the night staff, always moaning about how they're lazy, make mistakes and damage stock. Diesel says it's a load of bull and deletes emails from him, but Spencer's worried about getting in trouble and being fired. If he loses his job he'll run out of money, and he and Snowdrop will starve to death.

At 06.31 Spencer's cramming Red Bull into the fridge as fast as he can, when Bill taps him on the shoulder.

'Got to go now Spencer. I'm needed back at the super-store. It's just go, go, go.'

'Where is the superstore you work at Bill?'

'Where is it? It's... in... Do you know where the flyover is?'

'No.'

'It's near there.'

'Wait a minute!' Spencer jumps up. 'That's my X-wing Fighter.'

'This? Oh, so it is! How silly of me. You don't mind if I borrow it do you? I'll bring it back.'

Spencer shifts from one foot to the other. He'd rather not lend it out again, seeing as he's only just got it back from someone else he lent it to three years and—now—one-hundred-and-forty-seven days ago. Bill's got six mint condition Millennium Falcons though, so surely he'll look after it.

'I'll be here again tonight... most probably. Bring it back then. Hey, Warburton's just pulled in—you better go and help quick as you can.— Alright, catch you later.'

At 07.26 he's still stacking bread. They sell eight-hundred-and-fifty loaves on an average day.

'Hey, you don't need to do that Spencer. You should have left half an hour ago.'

It's Sinitta, one of the day shift stackers.

'Diesel wasn't here last night Sinitta. There was a man from the superstore near the flyover instead.'

'The superstore near the what?'

'The flyover. His name is Bill Poster and he's got six Millennium Falcons still in the boxes. He couldn't get the computer to work, and he said he had to read his newspaper and I had to do everything.'

'Is that right? Bill Poster... You go home now Spencer. I'll finish up here.'

'But I've still got to do the sandwiches, we're low on litre and half-litre semi-skimmed, Diet Coke, Volvic, Highland Spring, Buxton Water...'

'Spencer. Go home.'

'But what about the sandwiches and the litre and half-litre semi-skimmed? And we're low on Budweiser and Beck's.'

'Spencer! I won't tell you again.'

On the way out Maciek grins at him. 'I like your Lego. Very nice. Make big price. Very big price.'

'I told Bill Poster it's not for sale.'

'Bill? Oh sure, Bill.'

Spencer carries on. He's hoping to make the 07.58.

'Oh, and Spencer?'

Spencer spins round.

'Don't worry about the whisky delivery. Bill found out when it will come. Now fuck off home to Mummy.'

'I told you before, I don't live with Mum.'

Yes, definitely a whisky enthusiast he thinks, marching down the road, and looking forward to sitting on the train and daydreaming about the girl with long hair in the house with the boarded-up windows.

7

It's two days later, and thinking he heard the doorbell, Spencer stirs. He sleeps until 16.45 on the days after his first two shifts, but on this, the third day, he sets his alarm to thirteen-hundred hours, and that way he can get back into sleeping at night, even though he feels sleepy for much of that day. Now there's knocking on the door, and then louder, and Snowdrop hides under the bed. Spencer gets up and shuffles to the front door in his pyjamas. He's had an hour's sleep, on top of having worked flat out without taking lunch breaks for three shifts.

'Didn't you get my text?'

It's Robert, and Mrs Adeoye's standing next to him, her walkie-talkie crackling.

'What?' Spencer's not sure what's happening.

'Can we come in?' Robert asks.

Spencer doesn't say anything or move at all, but they come in anyway, and he follows them through to the living room.

'Please sit down,' Robert says to the policewoman. 'And open a window Spencer, it's like a furnace in here.'

'What's that white hair? It's not cat hair is it?'

'Yes, he's got a cat.'

'I don't want any cat hairs on me.'

'Is there something we can put on top of the chair Spencer? What about these magazines? They'll do.' He hands her a few, and she starts tearing out pages and laying them all over the armchair.

'That's my collection of *The Railway Magazine*.'

'Spencer, they're old. Mrs Adeoye can't get cat hairs on her uniform can she?' Robert shakes his head in disbelief.

Spencer shifts from foot to foot, flinching every time a page is torn.

Having ensured there isn't a millimetre of fabric left exposed, Mrs Adeoye carefully sits down, checking every angle as she does so, as if reversing a car into a tight space, her walkie-talkie crackling.

'I sent you a text about an hour ago Spencer,' Robert says, sitting on the sofa.

'I was asleep, and when I go to bed I change the profile on my phone to silent mode.'

'Spencer, we can't wait around just for you. Mrs Adeoye is a busy woman, and you're very lucky she could see you at all.' He shakes his head and looks up at the ceiling. 'Now, why don't you stop cluttering up the room in your pyjamas, put your dressing gown on, make us all a nice cup of tea, and come and join us.'

'Can he make tea?' Mrs Adeoye whispers loudly.

'He can.'

'Milk, two sugars thanks luv.'

Spencer shuffles out the room backwards, nodding repeatedly.

When he's back with the tea and the protocol biscuits, Spencer goes to sit alongside Robert on the sofa.

'Not there, Spencer. I need to put my paperwork there.'

Spencer sits on the chair at the table in the corner, and they make a start. To save time, they fill out forms as they go along, and Mrs Adeoye has two because Spencer isn't compos mentis, and Robert has to act on his behalf. First they have to go through address, full name, date of birth, emergency contact, things like that, and Mrs Adeoye writes very slowly and reads every word out loud, and Spencer's eyes keep rolling into the back of his head, particularly when Robert and Mrs Adeoye confer with each other, which is most of the time. Then there are the times when the walkie-talkie interrupts them with broken-up speech, and they have to wait until it's gone quiet again.

When it comes to the incident itself, and he's asked to talk about it, Spencer looks at his bare feet and doesn't say anything.

'Come on Spencer. You need to tell Mrs Adeoye what happened. She's a policewoman and if you withhold information you could get into trouble.'

Continuing to look down, Spencer wiggles his toes.

'Did they call you names luv?' Mrs Adeoye asks slowly and deliberately.

Apart from the occasional slurp, there's silence, and they all look at Spencer's toes. He can wiggle each one individually. When he's wiggled them from left to right three times, he blurts it all out. Mrs Adeoye keeps telling him to wait a minute, slow down, and asks how to spell some words, such as 'flick-knife' and 'retard'. Spencer tells her, but she doesn't seem to hear him and turns her head towards Robert each time.

'Well, that's good, but we don't have names or descriptions,' she says when she's got it all down, and read it out. 'You cannot say freckles nowadays. It's like saying a man is black. You cannot say that—Keep it away from me!'

Snowdrop has finally plucked up the courage to investigate what's behind the strange noises, makes a beeline for Spencer, rubs herself against his legs a few times and jumps into his lap.

'Yes, that's right,' Robert says, shaking his head. 'You can't say that Spencer. Do you understand? Wasn't there something else? Something distinctive... Jewellery, tattoos... scars?'

Spencer is silent, and they all look at his toes again—including Snowdrop—which have recommenced wiggling in sequence.

'What about the tracksuits?' asks the policewoman.

'Yes, you said they were wearing tracksuits. Do you remember the make... colour... anything at all Spencer. You're good at remembering details about trains. Tracksuits doesn't narrow it down, seeing as they're a uniform for the youth of today.'

It's true. Even Spencer wears them—under his anorak. When he first moved out of Sunrise he was still wearing the striped and check shirts, and corduroy trousers Mum chose for him. Robert said he looked like a deckchair, which was OK when you were on a beach, but not when you were in a high-rise far away from the sea, and he didn't fit into the community dressed like that, stood out like a sore thumb, and he didn't want that did he? So Robert had taken him shopping to JD Sports, and kitted him out in tracksuits and hooded tops, and donated his old clothes to charity. Mum said his new clothes made him look like a delinquent.

'I got my X-wing Fighter back Robert,' Spencer says, when they've stopped talking about tracksuits. 'But then Bill Poster from the superstore near the flyover borrowed it, and he didn't come back the next night or the night after that, and it might be missing.'

'It's only Lego Spencer.' Robert looks up at the ceiling. 'Mrs Adeoye has got enough serious crimes to investigate, without hunting high and low for toys.'

'It's one case per visit luv. I'm rushed off my feet as it is.'

'You've got plenty of other Lego sets.' Robert looks up at the ceiling again.

'Well,' Mrs Adeoye says to Robert on the doorstep, re-placing her hat, and ensuring there aren't any cat hairs on her, 'like I said, we'll check the CCTV, but I'm not holding out much hope, because it was dark and he said there wasn't any witnesses, and we haven't got any forensics to go on. They're all underage anyway—if it is those same kids—so our options are limited. I'll question them, as part of my enquiries—when I get a spare five minutes. I'll arrange for Victim Support to contact your lot as well.'

Feeling dizzy, Spencer holds onto the doorframe.

'It is them, Mrs Adeoye, it's Henderson and his cronies. Freckles, four or five of them; it all adds up. Well thank you for your time. Say thank you to Mrs Adeoye Spencer.'

'Thank you, Mrs Adeoye.'

Robert and Mrs Adeoye say their goodbyes, and Robert closes the door. 'I see you've been back to that house.'

'What house?' Spencer asks, following Robert into the living room.

'Don't play the innocent; you can't carry it off. I can read you like a book Spencer; you can't keep anything from me. That house.' He points at the pictures on the wall. 'The drawings you showed me before were black and white, so you must have been back there—and that was after I specifically told you not to. Well, what do you have to say for yourself?'

Spencer is silent.

'You're not to go there again. Do you hear? You don't want to go back to Sunrise do you?' He puts his paperwork in his canvas shoulder bag. 'I know what's best for you Spencer. Do you promise you won't go back to that house?'

Looking away, Spencer nods.

'See? That wasn't difficult.' He moves towards the front door, Spencer trailing behind, head bowed. 'And don't worry about Henderson and co. They won't bother you again. They're all mouth anyway, and like Mrs Adeoye said, you probably imagined the knife. It was dark after all, and the police carry out spot checks in this area.'

After Robert's left, and he's searched his reflection for words again, Spencer goes back to bed, because he can't seem to focus and everything's spinning, and it must be tiredness. Snowdrop joins him there, as if she too is tired from the ordeal, and having her fur vilified.

Almost immediately, the music starts up, and he knows he won't get any more sleep, so he goes into the bathroom, which is the quietest room when the people in 1819 put their music on loud—although the glass in the bathroom cabinet still vibrates—and he's slept in there before, and so has Snowdrop. But he knows he won't sleep this time, not after everything that's just happened. He closes the door, and it's completely dark in there on account of there being no window, and he sits with his back to the wall and hugs his knees, and rocks back and forth in time to the beat from downstairs.

His mind is blank for a long time, and it's nice, and he feels safe. But after a while he sees a door opening in his mind and a figure enters—no more than a dark shape—but he knows it's the one with the freckles, and he's going to cut him from mouth to ear. He hums as he rocks, and the black shape goes out and the door closes. But then the black shape comes back, keeps coming back. His hums grow louder and his rocks more forceful, and he's throwing his back against the wall, softly at first, and then with gusto. It seems to help, and after a while, although the black shape repeatedly comes in and out, it doesn't feel so bad, and then it doesn't matter. It even starts to feel good, as though the black shape is going to help him, and then he realizes why. The black shape is now a girl with long hair in a dress.

8

It's the same day and Spencer's on the track between the banks of wildflowers leading to the white house with the boarded-up windows, and he has his orange rucksack, big enough to fit a sleeping bag. It's May, and dog rose, columbine and forget-me-not have swelled the ranks, lending the banks a richer tone, and the wheat is taller and greener. Later in the day than his previous visits, the light is eggshell, the clouds egg-shape, white-edged and dark-centred, like eyes. He's left two bowls of food out for Snowdrop, he's brought the larger Tupperware box, and the poplars admit him with the rustling approval of their broad leaves.

A board is missing from each window, which no longer resemble Maciek's mouth, nothing like it, and he knows the girl with long hair in a dress is behind their removal. Just like the previous visits, he sits on the bench in the garden, except this time he has tea rather than lunch, although it's similar, because he couldn't bring hot food. He likes being here at this time, with the pink sun and the encroaching gloom. It feels different, thoughtful and wise, not just a glossy picture. He's always liked night-time, and sometimes he has the curtains open in his bedroom, and he and Snowdrop look at the twinkling lights spreading out beneath them. He knows it won't be like that here in the countryside, far from the city and streetlights. But he doesn't mind, because he's not afraid of the dark, and once he went on a survival weekend with a group from Sunrise, and he was the only one who stayed outside all night and didn't go back in the cabin, and everyone asked what it was like and said he was brave. It's getting cold, but he can always light a fire, because he bought matches —which made him feel guilty, because he isn't allowed matches—and the woods are nearby, and he has his torch. He's got a jumper in the rucksack, and he can wear that as well as his anorak inside the sleeping bag if he needs to, and he knows it's not going to rain because he checked the forecast.

Having finished his tea, he turns to look at the house behind him, and now the sun has gone down, and there's a little pink left in the sky, he can see it reflected in the black strips of glass, and warming the green-tinged paint. He feels he's never seen such beauty before, and the house teaches him new things every time he visits.

He thinks he will collect some firewood before it's completely dark, because the temperature will drop, and he should make a fire now rather than later, when he might have frostbite in his hands and not be able to strike a match. Pointing the torch ahead of him and from side to side, it shines on green eyes, and then a moving shape, and then nothing. Thinking it was a fox that smelt his pork pie, he's not scared, not at all. It's wet underfoot, and he's only got his plimsolls, which were fine for the track, but not so good for bogs—he didn't think of that did he? When his left foot is submerged and his sock is wet through with icy water, he gives up, because otherwise he might be sucked down to his waist and not able to climb out, and then he would die, although he's not quite sure what of, and Snowdrop would die of starvation.

So, he goes back, and he's cross with himself for not bringing spare socks or a towel, and he's been on a survival weekend and should know better.

He's already worked out where to sleep, and that's in the middle of the garden, where it's flat and it's just grass, although very long grass. It's only 20.48, and it's getting dark, and he's tired, having only slept an hour last night. Taking his anorak and over-trousers off, he lays them down on the grass, thinking there will be dew in the morning, and he doesn't want to wake up wet through and shivering. He keeps his tracksuit on though, and puts his jumper on, before climbing into the sleeping bag. He has nothing to use as a pillow, so he tears fistfuls of grass to pack under his anorak hood.

He reads his bus and trainspotting logbook and the number 37 timetable by the light of his torch, but after a few minutes he can't focus on the figures, and turns the torch off, and it's pitch black, and he giggles with excitement, and lies down. He used too much grass, and his head is propped at an angle and facing the house—now a silhouette—and there's light in one of the windows, and not in the others. The light goes fainter and brighter, and he knows it's coming from within, and a shape passed in front of it, and he knows the girl with long hair in the dress is in there and she's lit a candle. He can picture her sitting in the armchair, and her hair is straw-blond, like the girl in *Rumpelstiltskin*.

He likes that she's in there, and has lit a candle, because

ghosts and vampires wouldn't use them, and must be flesh and blood like him. He likes that she's there, and he hopes he will dream about her, as he turns sideways, presses his head hard against the grass pillow to flatten it, pulls the sleeping bag fully over himself and shuts his eyes.

★

Woken by shouting and a bright light in his eyes, Spencer tries to work out where he is and what's happening. But there's nothing to see apart from the light—which is like the sun in his face—and the black shapes of his fingers trying to shield his eyes.

'Oi! Oi you! You can't sleep here,' the voice is shouting.

It sounds like a girl's voice, and although he can't see her, it can't be the girl with long hair in the dress because she's nice, he knows she is, and it must be her evil sister, or another girl from somewhere else.

'Oi! I'm talking to you.'

Spencer feels a kick in his back.

'I said, you can't sleep here. Go on, get out.'

Another kick, and another and another, he's rolling over and over, and being kicked again and again, and he's entangled in something, something prickly, and it scratches his face, and he's trying to stand up or get out of the sleeping bag, but he can't, he's stuck, he can't even free his hands, and something's still entangling and scratching him, and he wonders if it's her, and she's a creature from the woods, covered in thorns. The light's on him and off him, and he hears the zip of his sleeping bag being pulled down, and he springs to his feet, except he has no shoes on, he can't see anything, he's wet himself and he's too scared to move. The whole time the evil voice is screaming at him to get out, and he goes into a ball, hands protecting his head in case there are more kicks.

'Look, there, in front of you. There's all your stuff. Well, what are you waiting for? Pick it up.'

He's on all fours and the light's in front of him, and his sleeping bag, rucksack, plimsolls and torch are all there, and he's putting the plimsolls on and grabbing his things.

'This way, this way,' the voice is shouting. 'Look, there's the path. Shine your torch on it then, go on.'

Fingers and thumbs, trembling with fear and cold, he can't seem to turn it on. The light is coming towards him, swaying from side to side, and then it's on him again. His torch is grabbed, turned on and shoved back in his hand.

'What is your problem? Are you a bit simple or something? Look, there's the path. Now, shine your light on it and get going. Go on!'

Spencer is kicked on his way, and then he's shining the light in front of him. He can't see the path though, that's the thing, and he's stumbling and falling, and his hands and feet are wet, and he's dropped his sleeping bag and rucksack, and all the time the voice is shouting at him, calling him names, saying he's useless.

He's on all fours again, his knees are wet—it's wet everywhere, there might be snakes, and he's petrified of snakes, and he's trying not to cry, but he can't help himself, because it's all gone wrong, and he thought the house and the girl were nice.

The light's on him again, shifting over him, faint to start with, and then honing in on his face and strengthening. The voice has gone quiet and the light is like the sun in his face, and he's grown accustomed to it now, and he doesn't hold his hands up, and it's liquid and rainbow colours through his tear-stained eyes, and he's crying uncontrollably now, and his face is strewn with dark water, blood and tears.

'You better come in,' the voice says quietly. 'You'll freeze your bollocks off out here. We'll get your things in the morning.'

Trembling and sobbing, he's helped to his feet, and, with an arm around him, led to the house, and, snivelling and sniffing, he discovers the girl isn't covered in thorns at all, and maybe, just maybe, when they get inside, he'll see she's wearing a dress, and have long hair the colour of straw, like the girl in *Rumpelstiltskin*.

They go in a door, and through the kitchen, which is dark and smells of cooking, and she's supporting him, and he's shaking, and his teeth are chattering, and he can see she's wearing dungarees, and her hair is short and black. They go through the hall, and he can make out there are pictures up and down the walls, and he's never seen anything like it, and she's saying, this way, this way, and into the living room, which is cosy and warm, with a fire crackling, and everywhere he looks there are candles in pots, and Spencer's never seen a prettier room in all his life, and he's stopped snivelling and sniffing, because the house is showing him nice, new things yet again.

'Come and sit by the fire. Sorry about that,' the girl says, 'I thought you were... Didn't realize you had... My goodness! Just look at the state of you! You wait there, I'll get a towel—two towels—and a basin of water. Then I'll heat some water up and you can have a proper wash.'

He looks around some more, and he wants this moment to last forever, because he knows she is the nice girl after all, and it doesn't matter what she wears or how she looks. She lives in this house in this special place, and that's all that matters. He likes everything in the room, and especially the fire, because he's never seen a fire in a house before, except in films and pictures. He likes the candle pots almost as much, or even the same amount, with the candlelight shining through the holes, some of which are star-shaped, and the dancing shadows on the walls and furniture.

When she comes back with the basin of water and towels, and helps him take his wet clothes off, she sees the bruises she inflicted.

'I'm so sorry about kicking you; I hope it didn't hurt too much.'

While she dabs at the scratches on his face with a sponge, which stings a bit—but he won't cry—and washes him, and dries him, and talks to him in a low voice, warm and crackly, like the fire, he looks at her. She's got nice teeth, and tattoos on her fingers—not bad ones like Maciek—strange shapes and letters.

'When I first saw you I saw red, and my instinct was I didn't want you here—not even in the garden, or anywhere nearby. I thought I wouldn't be able to sleep with you out there, even though all the windows are boarded-up, and the doors locked. Then I realized it wasn't right, it wasn't right at all, and it goes against everything I stand for.

'Anyway, what I'm trying to say is, you can stay the night. Well, you've lost your sleeping bag anyway—which is my fault, and I'm sorry about that—and you weren't able to find the path. I couldn't leave you out there to die of hypothermia. The trouble is, like I said, I saw red. I have a bad temper you see. I saw red and it took me a long time to calm down. Then, when I did calm down, I realized I was wrong. So, I'm really, really sorry about that.'

'What's your name please and thank you?' Spencer didn't hear any of that, and he's still looking at her, even though everyone tells him it's rude to stare, because he just can't help himself, and the girl doesn't tell him not to.

'Where are my manners! Goldy. What's yours?'

'Goldy!' Spencer laughs, and it's not a nervous laugh, or at least it doesn't seem like one. 'You've got black hair!' and he laughs some more.

'I know! It's a crazy old world isn't it?' She gets up. 'So, you must be called Brownie, because you've got brown hair—well, actually, it's got a bit of red on it as well,' and she dabs at the red bit with the sponge.

'My name's not Brownie, it's Spencer Frederick Morton.'

'Pleased to meet you Spencer Frederick Morton.' She shakes his hand. 'I'll get you some clean clothes, but won't bother with the hot water if that's alright with you, because it takes so long to heat up.'

Her bones make a reassuring click when she gets up, and he looks around the room some more; at the grandfather clock, at the bookshelves, at the light-fitting hanging from the ceiling with the plastic candles, plastic flames and plastic wax dribbles, and at the strange pattern on the rug, which he remembers seeing through the window that time. Maybe it has special powers, and the funny little shapes, some of which look like mythical beasts and magic symbols, relate to spells, and maybe Goldy's a witch, and she puts her hands in a certain place on the rug, and chants mystical words, and the tattoos light up, and she turns into a bat. He imagines he would never get bored of looking at the rug, the fire and the candles, and he might be happier than he's ever been in his life.

Later, Spencer's lying on the sofa, and he's wearing Goldy's clothes, and there are blankets on top of him, and Goldy's gone up the stairs to bed, and he thinks he's even happier than he was earlier. The candles have all been put out, but the fire's still orangey-red, and he can see the pattern on the rug, which looks as though it's different shades of blue and black, except for a strip in front of the fireplace, which has tiny traces of other colours.

He's very tired now, and, as Goldy said, he will sleep the sleep of kings, which he didn't really understand, but liked just the same, because it made him think of gold and silver, and precious stones like rubies, and the embers look like rubies, and they warm his heart.

9

It's the next day and Spencer doesn't want to come out from under the blankets into the cold, uninviting air, and neither does he want to be in this cold, uninviting room, with the cold light of day spilling in through the missing boards, painting white strips on the wall, and showing up all the dust and dirt. It's almost unrecognizable from last night: there's nothing cosy about it, and even the grandfather clock and the bookshelves look unfriendly, the rug is just a rug, the fireplace is ugly and grey, he can't imagine a fire being there, and the light-fitting in the ceiling looks like a grappling hook. He doesn't know what he would do if he did get up anyway, and doesn't think Goldy is up yet. He can't have a bath because she said there's no running water, and he can't use the toilets either, and she made him promise five times he wouldn't use any of them, and she gave him a cooking pot, but he hasn't used it yet, and he doesn't want to climb out from under the warm blankets into the cold, uninviting air to use it now either. Spencer doesn't remember being in a house with more than one toilet before, and this house has four, and, even though he can't use any of them, he can't wait to see them all. He can't wait to see the whole house, and Goldy said she'd give him a tour. He just wishes he'd had the tour last night, when there were probably candle pots with stars in every room. What he really wants though, is for her to come down the stairs and tell him what to do, because he doesn't know what the protocol is when you're in a big house in the countryside.

But what's that smell? There's a burning smell, and it's not the fireplace, which is giving off an old burning smell —it's a fresh burning smell—and he's worried that there's an actual fire somewhere, and he better get up and investigate, and he should move fast before the whole house burns down. So he gets out of bed, stumbles through the hall, and opens the door into the kitchen to start with, because that's the only other room he's been in.

'Morning, Spencer Frederick Morton,' Goldy says.

'Morning, Goldy Black Hair,' Spencer says, realizing that the burning smell is breakfast, and there's no burning at all.

The kitchen is so big—Spencer's never seen anything like it, except in films or telly.

'Sunny side up?'

Spencer looks out the window, and then at Goldy with a puzzled expression.

'Eggs, Spencer, I'm asking how you would like them fried—with the yolk runny or solid?'

Spencer peers into the frying pan perched on a camping stove, and back at Goldy.

'No, thank you very much. I have Rice Krispies and a glass of orange juice at breakfast and bedtime. I've brought them with me, and a bowl, and a spoon, and a glass. I've got some of that special milk that doesn't need to be kept in the fridge, and…' Then he remembers his rucksack is lost.

'Looks like you'll have to give Rice Krispies a miss today doesn't it? What about a bacon sandwich?'

'Yes please and thank you.'

'What about coffee or tea?'

'I don't have hot drinks, or alcohol. All I have is soft drinks, like orange juice, or Coke, or Pepsi, or Lemonade, or Fanta, or-'

'Alright, Spencer, I know what soft drinks are. Unfortunately, I don't have any, so you'll have to make do with water I'm afraid.'

Spencer doesn't know why she's afraid of water, unless maybe she nearly drowned or something, but it's soon forgotten when his eyes roam over the pots and pans, and crockery, and bottles covered in dust and spiders' webs. More than this he takes in the mould on the walls and the floor, the peeling paint, the dirt everywhere and the musty smell.

They bring their breakfast through to the living room, which Spencer is glad about, because being in the kitchen makes him feel a bit sick, and the living room's not nearly so bad, only a little bit bad. Spencer climbs back under the blankets, because he's cold, even with Goldy's fleece on, which is actually golden, like the golden fleece in the film, *Sea of Monsters*. Goldy sits on the rug, with a T-shirt on, because she thinks the temperature is fine.

'I'm going to level with you,' she says, putting her plate down and wiping her mouth with the back of her hand.

Spencer wonders if she means a level crossing.

'This isn't my house. I heard about a boarded-up house all on its own through a friend of a friend, and moved in two weeks ago. I was squatting in Greenstreet at the time and-'

Spencer giggles.

'Not that kind of squatting Spencer. It means living in an empty property scot-free.'

Spencer's heard this one before, although Scottish people, at least the ones he's met, have been alright.

'There were five of us to begin with in this two-bedroom house, and that was OK, that was manageable. But it never lasts. More people moved in. What happens?—I'll educate you in the noble art of squatting, seeing as you're a bit green about the gills. It's just an expression Spencer. What happens is, friends hear about it, and friends of friends, and passing acquaintances—it's impossible to keep a good squat under wraps. They're slippery though, these incomers, these bed 'n' breakfasters—yeah, that's what they pretend to be. They pitch up on the doorstep with some hard luck story, say they need a place to crash for the night, just one night. Well, one night becomes two, and then it's a week, and then you realize they're in with the brickwork. There were eleven or twelve by the time I left, which is crazy in a two-bedroom semi. It goes without saying, drugs had reared their ugly heads by then. Well, as soon as there's drugs—I don't mean hash of course—everything goes pear-shaped.'

Spencer's trying to take it all in, while watching Goldy's expressions and gestures, and the way she sips coffee and swills it about in the mug. The trouble is he's thinking about her name and her hair at the same time.

'So, yes, I heard about this place, and thought I'd give it a try. Naturally I kept it to myself, said I was staying with my sister in Wales for a bit.'

Wales was where Spencer went on the survival weekend, and he imagines Goldy and her sister sleeping outside.

'Anyway, to cut a long story short; because I'm squatting here, I can't stop anyone else from squatting either, do you see?'

Spencer doesn't see at all, but nods and turns the corners of his mouth up just the same.

'I thought you would have long hair the colour of straw, like the girl in *Rumpelstiltskin*, but it's not, it's short and black. Your hair *should* be the colour of straw, and not just because of the book, because your name's Goldy.'

'What is your obsession with names?'

'My name's Spencer and it has pence in it, and my hair's the colour of a one pence coin.'

'And that makes some kind of sense in Spencerworld does it? I'll tell you something about my hair and my name shall I? In fact, two things. One: my name is short for Marigold actually if you must know, not that anyone calls me Marigold anymore—except my mum when she's mad with me, which is quite often, now I come to think of it. Two: I had that Ladybird book as a child as well as you, and the miller's daughter didn't have hair the colour of straw, she had brown hair like yours. I remember it clearly because I wanted to be like her, and I had my hair braided to look like hers.'

She's got it all wrong and Spencer's shaking his head. He's got a good memory, much better than anyone else's, everyone says so.

'You're mixing up her hair with the piles of straw that the king commands her to spin into gold thread or she'll be bumped off. Then she marries him! Can you believe it? What message is that sending out to young children?'

She doesn't seem to be talking to him now, and she's cross about a king who isn't real, even Spencer knows that.

'Anyway, I remember that straw because it looked so pretty, and it was already golden—*and* it looked like hair. Do you see? You're mixing up the straw with hair, and even call it straw-blonde. Do you see, Spencer?'

Spencer's shaking his head furiously now. He doesn't like this at all, not one bit. He doesn't like it when people mix up his memories. That's even worse than someone saying they will come to your house at a certain time, and then being late, or even not coming at all, and he climbs out from under the blankets and runs out the room.

'Spencer! Where are you going?'

Why can't things be like you expect them to be? Why does everything have to go wrong all the time? If only she hadn't come out of the house and shined the torch in his face, then he could have carried on believing.

He's outside, and it's sunny and warm, but how can it be sunny and warm, when it's cold and dark in the house? Stupid, upside-down, dirty, disgusting house. He hates it now, and he's running fast to get the words and the stupidness of it all out of his head, except he hasn't got any shoes on, and he's treading on thorns and stones, and hopping about in pain.

'Spencer! Come back here. Spencer, get back over here this very second!'

He stops in his tracks, because she sounds just like Mum, and then he's trailing back to the house, muttering away to himself with his head down.

'We need to round up all your things for a start. What's that you're saying?'

'Goldy Black Hair, Goldy Black Hair, Goldy Black Hair…'

'What is your problem? Haven't you heard of Little John from Robin Hood? You need to come down from your cloud and live in the real world, where things don't always make sense.'

'...Goldy Black Hair, Goldy Black Hair, Goldy Black Hair...' He's going round in circles.

'How do you know my hair's natural anyway? Lots of women dye their hair. I bet Goldilocks dyes her hair.'

'Does not, does not, does not...'

'What about this? What colour's oil? Spencer! Spencer! What colour's oil?' She has to shout to be heard.

He's not listening, still going round in circles and chanting away. Until she grabs hold of the fleece.

'Answer the question Spencer. What colour's oil?' She holds him by the arms.

'Oil is black, oil is black, oil is black.' Avoiding her staring eyes, he works hard to free himself.

'That's right, oil is black. But did you know oil is also called "black gold"?'

He doesn't say anything, but, as he pants, he thinks about it.

'Well, it is. It's called black gold because it's valuable like gold. So you see, even though it sounds like a contradiction, like saying black white, something black can be compared to something gold. Do you see?'

Spencer's heard of contradictions, and he doesn't like them, tries to block them out, and wishes there were only black things with black names and gold things with gold names.

'Facts. Stick to the facts Goldy Black Hair.'

'It would be a pretty dull world if we stuck to facts and

called things by factual names all the time don't you think? What about art, literature, poetry? What about idioms and metaphors?'

Spencer knows about metaphors, and he doesn't like them.

'Like...' She tries to think of one. 'Like, "I wandered lonely as a cloud".'

'The Flying Scotsman; wheels: four-six-two, weight: ninety-six-and-a-quarter tons...'

'Is that what you do when you don't like something? Reel off train statistics?'

'...Length: seventy feet, height: thirteen feet, engine number...'

'Does that make everything better in Spencerworld? Is that your comfort blanket? Why's it called Flying Scotsman when it doesn't fly and it isn't a man? Answer me that.'

'You leave the Flying Scotsman alone Goldy Black Hair, you know nothing about it. Just because it's not scot-free. You hate Scottish people, you hate Scottish people, you hate Scottish people...' he sings in a high-pitched voice, and does a little dance.

'What are you on about?' Exasperated, she kicks the nettles. 'Anyway,' she says, sighing, 'we better see if we can find your things before they're sucked down into the swamp,' and she makes a noise like water going down a plughole.

Spencer chants and dances back inside, where he puts his plimsolls on, and during the search—which doesn't take long, on account of the rucksack being bright orange and the sleeping bag bright purple—Goldy answers her phone, and talks and talks on it, and doesn't pay attention to Spencer anymore, and he's left to think about things on his own.

She's still on the phone when they both go in the house, and she tells him to change into his clothes, which are in front of the fire, and bone dry, and he packs up his sleeping bag and puts it in the rucksack. Then she says she's got to carry on with the phone call, because otherwise heads will roll, and would he mind going now, and Spencer's a bit confused, but he doesn't argue, and they say goodbye, and he goes out the door, and it closes behind him.

He stands there for a bit, then walks past the living room window, and peers in through the gap, just like he did before, and she's sitting in the armchair, just like she was the first time he saw her, and it looks like she's wearing a dress again, but then he works out she's holding a cushion in front of her, and it's patterned, and looks like a dress through the dirty window. She's still on the phone, and shooing him away with her hand, and she looks cross, but he goes on staring at her through the window, and then she gets up, comes over and closes the curtains, and he can't see anything. He goes on standing there for a while, then leaves.

⑩

It's later the same day and Spencer's getting off the number 16 bus. He gets the number 16 when the number 37 terminates at the bus station, and it stops outside E block. As he's walking past the back of the bus shelter, he sees two track-suits through the burnt parts and graffiti, and he can tell they're teenagers from the way they're sitting, and he knows that teenagers often sit in bus shelters without catching buses. For a few moments he can't tell if they're the bad ones or not, because neither have freckles, and it's difficult to tell the other teenagers in E block apart, on account of all of them wearing tracksuits with the hoods up. The way he finds out they're the bad ones for certain, is that when one of them sees him, he draws a line across his neck with his finger, which is the death sign, and he's seen it in films. Both of them laugh, and it's not even dark, and there are lots of people around, but teenagers don't care about things like that.

Spencer runs, carries on running to E block, up the first six flights of stairs, stops, sits down, and pants hard. He can't get it out of his head, wonders if he ever will. He thought they were going to cut his face, didn't realize they were going to kill him, and Snowdrop as well, because she'll die from starvation.

The fact that it wasn't the one with the freckles makes it worse in a way, because it means they've talked about it, and all of them know he's going to die.

Tiptoeing up the remaining thirty-two flights, two for each floor, and counting them as he goes, his legs nearly give way eight times. He thinks that if it does happen, if they do kill him, he will be in such a state of petrification, he will die or faint from shock as soon as he sees the knife, but even this thought doesn't make him feel much better.

Snowdrop knows something's up as soon as he opens the door, because she runs away and hides under the bed, and not just a little bit under, all the way, and her eyes are big and round like the fox's in his torch beam.

★

It's later the same day, Spencer's scrubbed the mud off his shoes, tracksuit and sleeping bag, and washed them, and he's sitting on the bed with Snowdrop, and they're looking out the window.

When he came here, one of the first things he did was to move the furniture around so that he could see outside as he lay in bed. He especially likes to look at the view when the sun goes down, even though he can't see the sunset from his side of the building. He watches the street lights and car lights come on one by one, as the bits in between get darker, the sky changes colour, and sometimes stars come out. He doesn't think about much when he looks out the window, which is one of the things he likes about it, and how it calms him down. Every so often Snowdrop looks up at Spencer and Spencer looks down at Snowdrop, and then they both go back to looking out the window as the bits in between the lights grow darker.

Snowdrop likes to look out of the glass door in the living room as well, because the balcony's on the other side, and sometimes birds sit out there, especially when Spencer drops bits of bread out the kitchen window, which overlooks the balcony as well. Snowdrop likes to watch the pigeons, but not the seagulls, and hides under the bed when they arrive. Most of all she likes the sparrows, who can fly all the way up to the nineteenth floor despite being the size of a ping-pong ball. Sometimes when they hop about on the balcony she makes an a-a-a sound and dribbles, which means she wants to chase them. Spencer's not allowed to use the balcony— it's in his care plan—because he could fall off, even though it has railings; and the door's locked, and he doesn't have the key. There's a table and chairs out there, and a rusty swing seat that was left by a previous tenant which swings by itself and makes a squeaking sound when it's windy. There's lots of bird poo on the balcony, but no one can get out there to clean it because Robert says the key is lost and there's no way to get a spare one. Derek, who lives in 1616 has a key to his balcony, and his wheelchair can't even fit through the doorway. Sometimes it's open when he goes down there, because Derek likes the breeze, even though he can't feel it. Spencer asked Robert if he could go on Derek's balcony, but he said no, and changed the wording in his care plan to say he can't use any balcony in any building anywhere in the world, unless the building is on fire and the fire brigade have to use the balcony to rescue him. Robert said if there was a fire in E block, and the lifts were turned off, and he couldn't get down the stairs, nothing could be done for him because the fire brigade's ladders don't reach that high, and if he could break a window, he and Snowdrop would have to make a choice between their bones being smashed to pieces by jumping, or burning slowly.

Spencer continues to look out the window, even when the bits in between the lights aren't going to get any darker, and the people downstairs have put their music on loud. Tonight's the night they will keep it on all night, and Spencer's worked out they play loud music all night every other Thursday, although why they do this is a mystery. He doesn't mind the music so much when he's not trying to sleep, and if he's unable to get much sleep tonight, he can always sleep in the daytime and start preparing for his nightshift early, and anyway, whether he sleeps or not doesn't matter when he knows he's going to die. The funny thing is, now that he *does* know, apart from what will become of Snowdrop, he feels calm. He's not looking forward to being dragged to the place that smells of wee, and stabbed, and bleeding to death, but the 'being dead' part isn't so bad now he knows it's going to happen and there's nothing he can do about it.

Sometimes, if he keeps looking out the window at the city lights, he stops hearing the beat from downstairs, and it's like being asleep with his eyes open. He follows a car's lights on the motorway until he can't see them anymore, and then another, and another, and so on. There's a constant hum from the motorway, and, sometimes late at night he can hear one car if it's going very fast, even though the motorway is approximately four-point-two miles away.

Having this view is one of the best things about living

here, but he'd still rather live in a house in the countryside, like Goldy's house, which is what he's calling the white house with the boarded-up windows now, especially since it's no longer completely boarded-up. There it's quiet all the time, and the only sounds are the birds and the wind in the trees. It's got nice smells, and there are probably all kinds of animals other than foxes—and insects, plants and flowers. From this window it's buildings, roads and cars as far as he can see, and there aren't even any hills on the horizon, and the only nature is the birds on the balcony.

He's never stopped to consider these things before, and even when he's away from the house it's teaching him new things, and now it's making him think about the whole city. He was thinking about it earlier, when he was on the bus, looking at the houses going past the window. He's spent his whole life in the city, and never given it a thought. He's always liked the countryside though, and because his care plan says he should have regular exercise, and he doesn't know how to play sports, Robert said he could go on country walks, providing he wears appropriate clothing, keeps to footpaths and minor roads, follows the Countryside Code, doesn't walk too far and comes back the same day. His first walks were with a walking group from Sunrise, except he found them too slow, they spent more time in tea shops than walking, and Spencer doesn't like tea. The other thing was they always went in a minibus, and Spencer isn't so keen on buses that don't follow regular routes or keep to timetables.

He thought he was quite happy with this arrangement: living and working in the city, and going into the countryside once or twice a week. Now he's wondering what it would be like to stay there all the time.

Exchanging glances with Snowdrop, he wonders what she would make of living in the countryside, where there's a lot more birds, and she could chase them as much as she wanted to, and mice. She doesn't know any different to living in the tower block, but she's a cat, and it would be nice for her if she could go outside, even if it was just to sit in the garden.

Another thing he's been thinking about is apartment 1919, which he hasn't considered before either. When he moved out of supported accommodation and into his own home, he was so excited to have his own living room, kitchen, bathroom, hall, doors, windows, walls, floors and ceilings, he didn't stop to consider the possibility of living in another apartment or house. Ever since he came back today, in between thinking about being killed, or trying not to think at all, he's been thinking about 1919. When he walked into each room today it felt as though he was going into them for the first time. He doesn't think he's ever noticed that the walls are white and the carpets grey, just accepted everything, and never thought about making any changes. He always thought he liked being clean and tidy because that was what they taught him at Sunrise. He thought he liked hoovering, dusting, ironing, doing the dishes, putting the green duck in the toilet, things like that; but now he's wondering if it's really that important, and maybe he should be messier, have some tatty, old things, such as a grandfather clock, rugs with strange patterns and chipped mugs, and maybe he doesn't need to dust and hoover once a week. The thing is though, whatever he does to 1919, it could never look as nice as Goldy's living room, with the fire and all the candles. There's no fireplace here and his care plan says he's not allowed to have candles or matches, in capital letters.

The other thing he's wondering every now and then, as he and Snowdrop continue to watch the car lights going back and forth on the motorway, is what Goldy's doing.

11

It's the next day—or rather the same day, because Spencer and Snowdrop have been up all night. They tried to sleep in the bathroom, but that didn't work, and Snowdrop kept scratching at the door, which is a fire door, like most of the doors, and closes automatically, unless he wedges them open, except it says in his care plan the doors are, on no account to be obstructed under any circumstances. The only doors which don't close automatically are the bedroom and living room doors, and that's because they're obstructed by the carpet, which Robert says is a fire hazard, and he mentions it every time they have a meeting, except nothing is ever done about it. He uses a wedge for the bathroom door even though he's not supposed to, because there's no point in closing it when he lives alone. The only times he takes the wedge out is when he has an appointment with Robert, and when they're playing loud music downstairs and he's trying to sleep in there.

Spencer tried wearing his headphones, and listening to Stephen Fry reading *Harry Potter and the Order of the Phoenix*, but that didn't work, and he hasn't got a pair small enough for Snowdrop.

It wasn't so much the music that kept them awake, although that did keep them awake. It was more to do with worrying about the teenagers, and what they will do to Spencer—and Snowdrop too in a way, because if he dies, so will she. He wasn't feeling as bad about it last night, when they were looking out the window at the city lights, but that's because he wasn't thinking about going back to work, which means leaving the building. He thought it was safe going outside in the daytime, but if the teenagers can do the killing sign in the daytime, they can just as easily do the killing, and no one will do anything, the teenagers will have their hoods up, and the cameras won't be working.

It's alright today because he doesn't have to go out, and it's alright tomorrow morning and afternoon, because he doesn't have to go out then either, but at 17.30 tomorrow he has to go to work. If only there was a tunnel from the bottom of the building, and it wouldn't have to go all the way to the supermarket, just to the station would be enough. If there was a tunnel that led to the station, Spencer wouldn't need to worry at all, and he could come and go without fear. Well, he'd still be a bit scared on the stairs, especially below the third floor, and he might worry that the teenagers would discover the tunnel, but it would be better than the current situation.

Spencer's thinking about these things, and picturing the teenager making the killing sign, as well as the one with the freckles and scrunched-up face, and the knife glinting in the dark, and getting more and more worked up about it. Looking out the window in the daytime is nothing like the night because there's too much to look at, it's too busy, too noisy and there are no lights. In fact, looking outside in the daytime just makes him think about *going* outside. He's even taken the blue pills, which are for times like this, and they haven't made any difference.

When the music stops he's able to lie down on top of the bed, Snowdrop lies on his tummy and purrs loudly, and they can sleep.

★

It's later the same day, and they've been woken by the intercom. It keeps buzzing, so it must be important, and Snowdrop hides under the bed.

'Hello?' Spencer says into the intercom phone.

'Spencer, it's Mum,' the voice at the other end says.

He knows what she wants, and he still lets her in. It's 16.42 on a Friday after all, and in eighteen minutes it will be Friday evening. Another good thing about living here is that it takes at least five minutes for visitors to come up in the lift, and when it's Mum, that's enough time to hide his money. Robert's told him not to let her have any money, because it's not in her best interests, and he has to stick to his guns, which means he mustn't give in, and it's one of the few metaphors he likes, because sometimes he imagines shooting Mum. It was alright when he lived in Sunrise, where his money was kept in the office, and she couldn't get it, and she hardly ever visited him, but when he began independent living she visited a lot, and asked for money all the time, and Spencer gave in to her. Now he knows to say no, and anyway, he doesn't keep much money at home. He's not supposed to say he doesn't have any though, or he's lost his bank card, both of which he used to say. Robert's taught him to just say no, and that she should visit him because she wants to, rather than to borrow money. It took him a long time, but now he can do it. She's an alcoholic, and even though she always says it's for something else, she will spend the money on alcohol.

Standing on the doorstep, Mum has a cut on her lip and her hair's sticking up, and Snowdrop, who had just come out, runs back under the bed.

'Hello luv,' she says, kissing him on the cheek.

'Hello Mum,' Spencer says, closing the door slowly behind her.

'I'm gasping for a cup of tea.' She sits down. 'I brought some biscuits.'

Rummaging in her handbag, she brings out a quarter packet of custard creams, the wrapper tied in a knot.

'Thanks Mum.' He puts the biscuits on the coffee table. 'I'll make you a cup of tea.'

'You don't mind if I put the telly on do you?'

'No, but it's on the DVD channel,' Spencer picks up the remote control, 'so you'll need to-'

'I know how to use a remote control.' She snatches it off him. 'I might be old, but I'm not senile. You go and make the tea, there's a luv.'

Trailing out the room with his head down, he knows why she wants the telly on. It's so she can search for money without him hearing, because she knows when she asks for it he'll say no.

'How's work?' she asks when he comes back.

He tells her about Diesel being off, Bill Poster standing in for her, and how he's been rushed off his feet.

'That's terrible luv. Don't you let them take advantage

of you just because you're special needs, and if they do, just you tell them your mum will come up there and sort them out. No one takes advantage of my Spencer. You tell them that from me luv. Just going to the loo.'

He knows she'll rifle through his anorak and backpack on the way, and look in his bedside cabinet on the way back (not that she'll find anything) because he's watched her before through the crack in the door.

'Did I tell you about Sheila?' she asks when she's finally come back.

'Sheila next door? No Mum, no you didn't.'

'Well,' she says, taking her cigarettes out of her handbag, 'she had a heart attack- suspected heart attack anyway. An ambulance came for her.' Pausing to light up, she gets up, and stands in front of the window while she smokes. 'Well, she's in this ambulance, they're on the way to the Princess Royal, she's just had a heart attack- well, suspected—and do you know what she says to the paramedic who's in the back with her?'

Spencer doesn't know.

'She only says, "Excuse me dear, you couldn't stop off at the petrol station for me could you? Only I've just run out of me Regals." Can you believe it? To a paramedic, on the way to the Princess Royal, and she's just had a heart- suspected heart attack.'

She's looking out the window and the ash on her cigarette is getting longer. Spencer used to ask her not to smoke, because it's not his property, and neither's the furniture or the carpet (in case she burns a hole in something) but she used to say she wasn't going all the way down to the ground floor for a fag was she, when by the time she came up again, she'd want to go down for another. Now Spencer doesn't bother, and she just lights up.

'Well, as you can imagine, the paramedic wasn't having it. Against the rules, he says. Well, do you know what she did then? She only starts screaming, pulling the tubes out of her, getting up off the stretcher. Can you imagine?' She laughs. 'Rick—he was in the ambulance with her—and the paramedic try to restrain her. But you know what she's like when she gets going. She grabs this paramedic by the throat. Rick's trying to get her off, but then he falls over, and he's rolling about on the floor, because they're going round a roundabout. So in the end, they stop for her, and Rick jumps out and gets twenty Regals. Rick told me about it the next day.'

She takes a long drag and the ash falls on the floor. That's one good thing about having a grey carpet, thinks Spencer, now he's noticed the colour.

'I'll just flush this down the loo.' She hurries out the door. Again she's ages. 'The thing is luv, I'm a bit behind with the rent this month, and they said I had until tomorrow to pay up or I'd be out on my ear, and you don't want your old Mum living on the streets again do you?' She says all this quickly and she's pacing up and down, and wringing her hands.

'Mum-'

'I'm really desperate, Spence, honest I am—I wouldn't ask otherwise. I'd ask your brothers and sisters, only none of them are talking to me. Fifty quid, that's all I need, just to see me through to Monday, then I'll be able to get an advance on my dole money, and I can pay you back.'

Spencer looks at his feet poking out of his pyjama bottoms and wiggles his toes.

'Just this once Spence. Be a luv. I promise I won't ask you again. Spencer? Luv?'

Spencer tries to make his mind blank.

'Alright, thirty then, just to see me through to Monday.' She's pacing all over the room now.

'Come on Spence. This is the last time.'

'Have you been to AA lately Mum?' Spencer's staring hard at the little toe of his left foot, which is wiggling manically.

'What did you- Did I hear you right?' She's stopped pacing, and out of the corner of his eye, Spencer sees her arms are going up and down like a jack-in-the-box. 'How could you say that? You know I've stopped drinking. I haven't had a drop in six weeks.' She's pacing again. 'Even my own son doesn't believe me... My own flesh and blood...'

Spencer wonders if anyone's toe's fallen off through wiggling it too much.

'After all I've done for you. I was in labour for thirty-six hours with you. All the others shot out—shot out like champagne corks they did—but you, oh no, you had to be difficult.'

Spencer wonders if Goldy can wiggle her toes independently like he can.

'Fed you, changed your nappy, clothed you... All those things I did for you for years—and this is how you repay me?'

'Robert said...'

'Oh, here we go. I don't care what Robert said. Jumped up little...' She lights another cigarette. 'He doesn't have to do any actual work does he. Just tells people what to do. He doesn't actually do anything himself does he. Interfering…'

'Mum, I'm not allowed to give you any money.'

'Robert said… I ask you.' She's pacing up and down again and can't seem to decide what to do with her arms. 'Twenty then. Twenty and I'll go.'

Spencer continues to stare at his toes, although the life has drained out of them and they're about to drop off one by one.

'Alright, ten. Nice crisp tenner and I'll be out of here.'

Spencer is whispering something.

'What's that you're saying? Just tell me where it is Spence—I'll help myself, and I promise I'll just take ten. On my life.' She's standing still now, facing him, inhaling big gulps of nicotine, and it could go either way.

'…designer: Nigel Gresley, built: 1923, retired: 1963…' He's audible now.

'Oh here we go. Trains! My youngest son… Apple of my eye… cares more about fucking trains than his own fucking mother.'

The swearing has started, and when the swearing starts, the fists are sure to follow.

'…builder: Doncaster Works, operator: London and North Eastern Railway…'

He can't hear her now because he's shouting, his fingers are in his ears, his eyes are closed and he's rocking back and forth. He carries on like this until he hears the front door slam, and then he carries on some more, and when he's finished the Flying Scotsman, he goes on to the Mallard, which looks nicer, but isn't as interesting because it's no longer in service.

When it's safe, he slowly opens his eyes, takes his fingers out of his ears and breathes deeply ten times, and then opens the kitchen window. She didn't hit him, that was something—and maybe she's been going to the anger management sessions—although the coffee table's upside down. Coaxing Snowdrop out from under the bed, he has to show her inside every room and, once satisfied, she sits on Spencer's lap, where they both stare at the undrunk tea, and the uneaten custard creams, the wrapper tied in a knot. After a while, Spencer pours the tea away, and, stamping on the biscuits with all his might, he empties the crumbs out the window, and they watch pigeons peck at them.

12

It's the next day, Spencer and Snowdrop were up all night and slept in the daytime again—not one big sleep—broken bits, like the custard creams. The one good thing about Mum's visit was that he stopped thinking about the teenagers while she was there, and afterwards, when he was worrying how she'd get some money. He's also been thinking about how long she was in labour with him, which is different every time, and Spencer remembers these things. He's noticed that the more worked up she is, the longer she says it was. The other thing is what she said about having to feed him and everything. Gran said she did all those things and Mum didn't change one nappy, because she was an alcoholic even then, and Gran looked after all his brothers and sisters as well. He can't ask Gran about it anymore, not now she's in Heaven.

Robert told Spencer he has to lay down ground rules with Mum otherwise she'll take advantage, and that's why he can't lend her money or let her stay with him again. Robert said he can't help Mum himself, and can't even make a referral, because not only does she live in a different unitary authority, but her problems are substance abuse and Robert does learning disability.

He's stopped thinking about Mum, and he's back on the teenagers, seeing as it's nearly time to go to work. Every now and then, when he's preoccupied with getting ready, he forgets about them for a bit, and then remembers, and the knife goes in his tummy again. If only he could have a suspected heart attack like Sheila next door, and call nine-nine-nine; then he would be taken down in the lift by paramedics, and they'd protect him from being stabbed. He thinks you have to be old though, to have a suspected heart attack.

No, what he's got to do is knock on Mrs Jenkins' door and ask her if she'll accompany him in the lift, because he's even too scared to go down the stairs. He's scared just walking from room to room, and his legs are like jelly, and that's just thinking about it, in his own home with three locks and a chain on the door. If he went down the stairs in this state he might fall, and break his neck.

He's even petrified going out the door, in case he sees a teenager in the corridor, and he doesn't know how he will cope if he sees a tracksuit and baseball cap, and it could be Mr Higgins, the keep-fit fanatic, and he's seventy-eight. After he's read the Going to Work List on the back of the front door out loud four times and checked his keys are in his pocket eight times, he opens the door more quietly than ever before, and, like quicksilver down the hall, Snowdrop disappears into the bedroom.

Mrs Jenkins doesn't answer the door, and Spencer worries *she's* had a heart attack, until, furtively glancing from side to side, he sees the top of an old lady head through the glass part of the door to the lobby.

'Oh Spencer, it's you. I wonder if you wouldn't mind accompanying me in the lift again, only I dropped my last egg on the floor.'

Spencer laughs—a nervous laugh.

Once out the building, and along the path—where she points out dog dirt, syringes and a condom—he stays with her until they're on the road, before doubling back to the station.

When he walks through the swing doors at work, Diesel's in her chair.

'Alright Sp-'

Spencer's too excited for pleasantries, small talk, and 'how's it hanging?'

'There was a man here last week. Diesel. and his name was Bill Poster, and he was here on the first shift, but not on the other two—there was no one here on the other two—and on the first shift—the one Bill was at—he couldn't get the computer to work, and I had to walk up and down the aisles with a notebook and an HB pencil, and write down everything we were short of, and I filled up the notebook, and the margins, and the bits at the top and bottom of the pages, and I had to take down all the boxes myself, because Bill had to read a newspaper, and I think he's a slow reader, because it took him all night, and I was rushed off my feet, and-'

'Spence... Spence... Hold your horses.'

Spencer knows this means he's talking too fast, but he still doesn't like it because it makes him think of horses, and he's afraid of horses.

'Let's go back to the start. What was the man's name?'

'Bill Poster, and he came from the superstore near the flyover, and-'

'T-t-t-t.' Interrupting, she waves her arms. 'For starters, Bill Poster is a made-up name.'

'But, he said his name was Bill Poster, and-'

'Uh-uh-uh-uh... Forget the name Bill Poster. Do not say the name Bill Poster again. Bill Poster is fictitious, he does not exist.' She waves her hand as if she's made him evaporate. 'As for a flyover, I've lived in this city fifty-six years and I've never heard of a flyover in my puff. He was pulling your leg.'

Spencer doesn't like this one either. 'But he borrowed my X-wing Fighter, and I only just got it back from Norman Beazley, who borrowed it for three years and one-hundred-and-forty-six days, and I brought it in to show you, but Bill—the man—saw it, and asked to borrow it, and he's got six Millennium Falcons and they're still in the boxes.'

'Ah... *now* we're getting somewhere. He's pulled a fast one. Don't worry Spence, I'll get my people onto it and we'll track down this rogue. He's probably working for Darth Vader.' Getting up, she makes a shimmying motion and pulls her belt up, setting all her keys jangling. 'Meanwhile, back on Planet Earth, life carries on—but not as we know it... I've loaded up the wagon for you. I'm off for a fag.'

He's thinking about Darth Vader as she passes, then notices her face for the first time.

'You've got a black eye, Diesel.'

'Have I?' Stopping in the doorway, she feigns surprise.

'Yes you have. It's yellow here, black here and green there- oh and there's a bit of purple just here.' He points to each colour.

'Well I never.'

Spencer gets to work. He likes his job, uniform, name

badge, and he likes stacking shelves. He knows what he has to do and where everything is, there's a structure, and there are rules which cannot be broken. Unlike so much of the world, there are no grey areas, no confusion, and no phrases or jokes that don't make sense. Another good thing about his job is that it keeps his brain occupied and stops him from worrying about things. He was actually looking forward to work for this very reason. When he was in 1919 he couldn't stop thinking about the teenagers, but here he has to concentrate too much to let them into his head. It's just *leaving* 1919 that's the problem, and that's why he worries about the teenagers when he's *in* 1919.

As he's putting cans of Red Bull in the fridge, he allows his mind to wander, but only in the direction of Bill Poster. Well, there's a funny thing; he doesn't exist, and if he doesn't exist he must be a ghost. He didn't look like a ghost, although then again, maybe that's why he didn't lift any boxes—because he knew he wouldn't be able to. Spencer only saw him lift a newspaper, and newspapers weigh practically nothing. No, he did lift the X-wing as well, but that's only thin plastic, and surely a ghost would be able to manage that. There's no such place as the flyover either, and maybe he's not working for the Empire after all, and maybe he comes from a supermarket in a parallel universe, like in that episode of *Star Trek Discovery*. Thinking about parallel universes hurts his head, and he prefers to think Bill's a ghost.

He quite likes the idea of a ghost having borrowed his Lego model, and perhaps he's taken it to the spirit world, and maybe famous people from the past will get to see it, like the train designers Richard Trevithick, George Stephenson and Nigel Gresley. It would still be nice if he could have it back though, after they've seen it.

'Did you hear about Maciek?' Diesel asks, not looking up from her phone, when he returns to the warehouse.

Spencer hasn't.

'Got the sack for half-inching a bottle of Smirnoff. Caught on camera putting it down his trousers. Took it right off the shelf, the moron.'

Spencer doesn't know what to say, mainly because he hasn't fully understood what Diesel just said.

'Thanks to your tip-off I think we might be seeing our Polish friend next week, during the next whisky delivery.'

Spencer still doesn't follow, although he knows better than to ask when Diesel's playing a game on her phone. He understands Maciek's lost his job, but that's about it. He thought she said he put a bottle down his trousers, which doesn't make sense, so it must be a saying he's not familiar with. As for whisky, he already knew Maciek was an enthusiast, so surely that's why he's coming back for the delivery.

In his lunch break, rather than poring over the *Buses Yearbook*, he does his grocery shop, using the list he's been adding to over the last week. He has healthy dinners that he learned from an independent living course at college Julie used to take him to (all of which can be prepared with plastic cutlery) and has a certificate to prove it. He always buys exactly what's on the list, no more, no less, and when something isn't available, he goes without. Tonight, however, down the meat aisle, and noticing the bacon, he thinks Goldy might like some, and picks up a Danepak streaky, the same kind she had, and then seeing it's 'buy one, get one half-price', he takes another. Then he thinks it would be nice to buy some eggs for her. Then he thinks it would be nice to get her something special, so, after much deliberation, he settles on a three-hundred-and-eighty gram box of Terry's All Gold Dark.

Later, he sees three tracksuits with their hoods up in the medicine and men's grooming aisle, and his first thought is it's the bad ones and they know where he works. Caged animal coiled, he watches them round the corner, from where their faces can't be seen. Standing there several minutes, they open boxes, take bottles out, put them back and snigger. When they've left the aisle, and—watching from a safe distance—the store, he goes over to the boxes. It's easy to see which ones they picked up, because they're not lined up and the labels aren't front-facing. Opening a box of haemorrhoid cream, he's surprised to find condoms. Unearthing several more boxes containing misplaced condoms, he continues his investigations in the condom section, where he discovers tampered boxes, torn cellophane, and finds a tube of haemorrhoid cream inside one, and wart ointment in another. Rehousing the undamaged medicines in their original boxes, he takes five opened boxes of condoms, which can't be sold, back to the warehouse for Diesel to log.

'Got a hot date?' she asks.

He turns his mouth up at the corners, which seems to be the response she's after.

Putting out the newspapers at six, Aggie and Jean are leafing through the women's magazines. He's wondering when Aggie's going to ask him about stripy paint, elbow grease, or something else they don't sell, but she doesn't notice him.

'Did you see Diesel?' Jean asks Aggie.

'Oh, is she back? Something the matter with her?' Aggie asks.

'She's got a black eye. I heard it was a lover's tiff.'

Sniggering, they continue flicking through *Closer* and *Heat*, reading out snippets to each other.

After they've gone—and as Spencer puts the magazines back in the right places, and straightens up the edges of all the magazines—which isn't his job, he just likes doing it—he mulls over what they were saying about Diesel. He didn't even know she had a husband.

He's not so worried about seeing the teenagers on his way home from work, and takes the lift, because he doesn't think teenagers get up early in the morning.

13

It's two days later—or is it three? Spencer's still confused about that one. He's finished his third shift, he's had a small sleep, he's got his orange rucksack on his back, he's marching along the yellow road to Goldy's house. The tops of the clouds are so bright they appear to be etched in light, while the lower portions are as sensual as silk underthings.

He doesn't have to worry about the teenagers for the time being, because Mrs Jenkins' son is staying with her after his wife left and he suffered a nervous breakdown. Thomas used to be a boxer, and has problems controlling his temper, but he's nice to Mrs Jenkins, and when she told him about her and Spencer being afraid to go down in the lift on their own, he said it was his duty to act as their bodyguard day and night, and if anyone so much as gives them a dirty look he'll knock seven bells out of them, and then started crying over something else entirely. Spencer has discovered he's a man of his word, and has even been waiting for him on the main road when he's due back from his shift.

Something else that's been going well is that he might get his X-wing back. Diesel found a 1999 model on eBay selling for five-hundred pounds. At first, Spencer didn't see how it could be the same one, because Bill has only borrowed it, and the seller's name is Gordon Briggs, and when Diesel looked through the seller history, there were no other *Star Wars* models, and only things called bongs, shisha pipes and protein powder. Diesel made some phone calls and found out there's a Gordon Briggs at the Coldwater store, and left a message for him, saying that if he didn't return the X-wing to its rightful owner within twenty-four hours she would call the police. Spencer wondered why she mentioned the police, although he knew not to ask, and if he gets his model back he'll be thrilled.

When turning off the road and stepping carefully down the track, Spencer notices a frog jump in front of him, and then another, and another. He sees dragonflies darting about too, their wings shimmering in the sun; and all the frogs and dragonflies seem to be going the same way as him, as if mini Thomases were protecting him.

More gaps have appeared in the boards, and the house looks happier somehow, and that must be because it's no longer abandoned, and lived in again. Goldy doesn't come out when he knocks on the back door, or on the front door, or any of the windows on the ground floor, so he calls her name, and throws stones at higher windows. He wonders if she's listening to music with headphones, and tries to push both doors, but neither budge. He feels a bit sad, because he's been here ten minutes, and already the house doesn't look quite so friendly. Then he wonders if perhaps Goldy is a ghost too. Whether she is or not, he decides to wait for her, and build a fire to keep warm if she still hasn't appeared when the sun goes down, and he hasn't brought his sleeping bag this time.

He's got his walking boots and matches, and treks to the trees in search of dead wood. Stepping from tussock to tussock, he makes it without getting his feet wet, returning with an armful of varying thickness. Spencer knows how to make a fire, having learned about it on the survival weekend, except they had paper and firelighters. Then he remembers the Metro newspaper in his rucksack, and, crumpling it into balls, he manages to light the fire and keep it going. Feeling hungry, and, apart from the presents, only has an apple and half a packet of peanuts, so, reluctantly, he decides to cook some eggs and bacon. Looking round for something to use as a frying pan, he makes do with a bit of slate, throwing it into the fire. Laying bacon on it isn't a problem, but the first two eggs slide off, even after cracking the second one between the rashers. Positioning another slate alongside the first, and attempting to arrange stones around the edge, he's thwarted by the heat, gives up, and lays down another couple of rashers.

When they're cooked, and picked up with two sticks, he lays them on his rucksack until cool enough to eat. Barely edible, they taste of smoke, but go towards filling a hole, along with the apple and remaining peanuts.

It's grown dark, save for a rim of yellow fire burning around the edge of the sky. The temperature is dropping, and, moving closer to the hearth, he wishes he'd used his rucksack to transport more wood.

The house looks miserable and cold. Maybe Goldy's had an accident, tripped up on junk, fallen down the stairs, she's in a coma or dead, and lying in a pool of blood with flies buzzing about and laying eggs on her. Or maybe she's fine, but doesn't want to see him, doesn't like him anymore, hates him.

Marching up and down to keep warm other thoughts circle. What if Thomas gets bored of escorting him in the lift? What will he do then? Or what if Thomas thinks Spencer gave Mrs Jenkins a dirty look when he was just concentrating and it made him frown? Would Thomas knock seven bells out of *him*? Then there's this business with the X-wing. What if Diesel is only pretending to help him because she wants to keep it, or wants to sell it on eBay herself?

Marching or standing still and shifting from foot to foot, when sitting back down he wiggles his toes as much as his boots will allow.

'Hello,' a voice says out of the darkness.

Spencer jumps up, as well as nearly jumping out of his skin.

When close enough to be lit up by the embers, he can see it's Goldy, she's wheeling a bicycle and smiling.

'Hello Goldy. I've been waiting for you.' He draws closer himself.

'I can see that.' She's still smiling, the embers glowing in her eyes. 'Let's go inside. If you'll give me a minute—I have to get in myself before I can let you in.'

Spencer is about to ask what she means, but she's disappeared, reappearing several minutes later behind the opening back door, and he brings his rucksack inside.

'How did you do that?' He's amazed.

'Squatter's secret.' She taps her nose.

He can't wait to give her the presents and show her the book he's brought, but has to wait until she's lit a few candles, and shovelled up his fire and rebuilt it in the hearth, and gone to the kitchen to heat up soup for them, which they have with bread in front of the fire.

The moment she puts her bowl down, and doesn't appear to be going anywhere, Spencer starts up, going at it nineteen to the dozen.

'I've brought you some things Goldy.' He hands them to her one by one from his rucksack without looking up. 'This is some eggs for you, but I'm afraid I tried to fry two on a slate, and now there's four. This is some Danepak streaky bacon for you, but I'm afraid I fried four rashers and there's twenty left. This is some Terry's All Gold Dark chocolates for you, and I haven't had any of them, and you can tell I haven't because the box is wrapped in cellophane. They must be your favourite chocolates because they're gold like your name and dark like your hair. This-'

'That's so sweet of you. You really didn't need to. Mmm... I love dark chocolate.'

Spencer feels warm inside.

'You should buy free-range eggs though.'

'Free range eggs.'

'Yes, where the chickens can roam about freely and aren't inside cages.'

Eggs are eggs, thinks Spencer, but lets it go when, gazing around the gloomy interior, he thinks of something else.

'Next time I'm going to bring you candles, because it looked much nicer before when there were twenty-eight.'

'So this is going to be a regular event is it—you turning up when you feel like it? Don't I have any say in the matter?' Her face is serious.

'I... I... You said I could squat here like you Goldy Black

Hair. You did. I don't forget things. You said it, and it's not nice to change your mind.'

'I'm joking you giant twit.' Laughing, she exposes her throat.

'Joking, yes, joking.'

'I can see I'll have to watch what I say to you. But as for the candles, it's very kind of you, but you really don't have to.'

'It's alright because I get a fifteen per cent staff discount, and boxes of tea lights are on buy one, get one half-price. I just want it to be like it was before.'

'Nothing can ever be like it was before. Everything happens at a particular time for a particular reason, and every second is different from the last. One second you're a big fat pheasant, the next you're shot out of the sky. The Earth is spinning, tectonic plates are shifting,' and pointing at their imagined passage down her arm, 'corpuscles are flowing. Nothing stands still. Didn't you know that?'

Spencer didn't know that, and he's never heard the like, and he's fascinated—by the thought of her corpuscles as much as anything else—whilst at the same time liking the sound of her words, because they're so definite. But he doesn't know what it's got to do with candles and he's still going to buy the tea lights.

'I've brought something else to show you Goldy. This is my favourite book and it's called the *Golden Treasury of Trains*, and it was Grandad's when he was a boy, but he's gone to Heaven. Grandad gave it to Dad when he was a boy, but he's gone to Heaven as well.' Each time he says 'Heaven', he turns his mouth down at the corners. 'Dad gave it to me when I was a boy, and I've still got it. It should be your favourite book as well, because of the word golden.'

'Can't argue with that. Listen, I'm just going to make a coffee, and then we can get started on the chocolates.'

Leaving him with the *Treasury* open in his lap at the marbled endpapers, she takes her phone to light her way, but he can't wait, and follows her into the kitchen.

'It's got all the famous trains in it going back to Stephenson's Rocket, which was designed by Robert Stephenson in 1829. It had a zero-two-two wheel arrangement and it's top speed was thirty mph—which stands for miles per hour—and it doesn't sound very fast today, but in 1829 it would have been very fast, and that's why they called it the Rocket.'

Carrying on like this, he doesn't notice Goldy looking at her phone. When she's made the coffee, and they've gone back to the living room, he carries on without barely taking a breath. She has three chocolates, and keeps offering him the box, but he's far too excited. While he rattles through the rolling stock of the 1800s, she returns to her phone.

'This is the *Coppernob*, one of my all-time favourites, built in 1849-'

'Listen Spencer, I'm not really in the mood for your *Coppernob*, if that's alright with you,' Goldy says, now that her phone is down to ten per cent.

'But…'

'Would it surprise you to know I'm not actually all that interested in trains?'

Spencer is lost for words.

'Let me put it to you another way. Imagine if I showed you a book. The Golden Treasury of… Let me see… Horse Brasses. Yes, that's it, the *Golden Treasury of Horse Brasses*.

Imagine I was mad keen on horses, and horse brasses in particular. Imagine if I showed you all these pictures of horse brasses and went on and on about them, and you didn't get a word in. What would you say to that?'

Spencer is too shocked to think about horse brasses right now, and he carries on looking at the Treasury, and running his fingers over the beautiful illustration of the *Coppernob*.

'I don't think you'd find it all that interesting would you?' and she gets up. 'Listen, after I go for a pee, I'm off to bed. Your bedding's still over there.'

When she's returned, Spencer's already tucked up safe and sound, and he's still clutching the Treasury without realizing it.

'Listen Spencer. I say what I think, and it won't always be what you want to hear. Don't worry, you'll get used to it. If you go outside in the night, don't forget to lock the door when you get back. 'Night.'

'Goodnight.'

It's the first word he's uttered since he was discussing the *Coppernob*.

It doesn't make sense. How could she not like the Treasury? It's almost got her name in the title. It's such a beautiful book as well, and he's holding it to his heart, beating as fast as a locomotive going flat out downhill. It has a green cover with fancy gold writing pressed into the surface, like a railway cutting. It's the most beautiful thing in the world—well, apart from the actual locomotives themselves—oh yes, and apart from this very room he's in right now, when it had twenty-eight candles and the fire crackling.

As he watches the embers going dull, he thinks some more about her not liking trains, and he still can't accept it.

It's like trying to imagine space going on forever—he just can't do it. He wiggles his toes and the caged animal is up to its old tricks, and he can't stop thinking about it. But then he imagines taking her on a steam train, and he'll teach her all about them, and little by little, she'll start to like them, and then love them as much as he does. Presently, the *Treasury* rises and falls slower on his chest, and his toes stop wiggling.

14

It's the next day, and, sitting cross-legged in front of the fire, having just finished breakfast, Spencer's been telling Goldy about his X-wing, and how Diesel's helping him get it back.

'Have you got to be anywhere?' she asks, flicking the smouldering wood over with the poker and tossing another log on.

'No, I'm on my days off today, tomorrow and approximately threequarters of Thursday.'

'Good, neither have I, but hopefully this won't take quite as long as that. You and I are going to try a little experiment.'

Satisfied with the fire's sound effects, she gives him her full attention, to which she already has his, hook, line and sinker.

'This is how it works. You ask me a question that you really want to know the answer to, and I provide the answer, which might take anything between a second and... let's keep it to five minutes. But here's the important bit Spencer.' She claps her hands. 'You listen carefully to what I have to say, and then, when I stop talking, you ask another question, which my answer brings you to. Do you understand?'

Spencer doesn't, but eager to give it a try, and more to the point, please Goldy, he nods vigorously.

'Good. Now, while I powder my nose and make more coffee, I want you to think up a good question, that is about me, and which I will enjoy answering and you will enjoy listening to.'

He watches her pick up toilet paper and washbag, unbolt the door and slip behind it.

When she returns with a fresh mug and sits back down, again his eyes follow every movement.

'I've thought of a question, Goldy,' he says, pleased with himself.

'Ask away,' she says, taking a slurp.

'Have you ever been on a steam train?'

The contents of Goldy's mouth shoot out.

'I've really got my work cut out and no mistake. I can see now I overestimated your entry level. Let's get back to basics.'

Putting her mug down, she clears her throat, and Spencer awaits further instructions.

'Often, when two people meet each other socially, and they're going to spend some time together, they ask each other certain questions. It's a social convention. Primates are sociable, and, when in a relaxed social setting, they want to bond with each other.'

Spencer tries to picture these primates Goldy speaks of in a setting, such as up a tree or in a forest clearing.

'You see, we want to find out if we've got things in common, and if there's going to be benefits from associating with each other. So, we ask each other certain questions, such as: what's your job?, where do you live?, where did you grow up?, what are your interests?... er... what do you like to do in the evenings? That sort of thing. Do you understand?'

Spencer nods vigorously.

'So, shall we try again? Ask me another question.'

'What's your job?'

'*Now* we're getting somewhere.'

She rearranges her legs, and Spencer, still cross-legged, puts his elbows on his knees and rests his chin on his hands.

'I don't have a job anymore, but I used to, and it was the most amazing job in the world.'

Spencer's eyes grow big at the prospect Goldy used to be a train timetable compiler.

'I'll start at the beginning. My parents are wine lovers. They were always buying different types of wine, and they would talk and talk about the grape, the vintage, the bouquet, the palette... I could go on. My sister and brothers weren't interested, but I caught the bug. Even before I was allowed to drink, I would sniff my parents' wine, taste it and spit it out. I was like a sponge, and because my parents were so passionate, I learned a great deal even before I came of age. Anyway. As soon as I turned eighteen, I got a job as a waitress—I loved food almost as much as wine. Well, because I was so knowledgeable about wine, and talked about it with such confidence, I would advise customers on what wines would go well with the food they ordered. I soon earned a bit of a reputation, and people would seek out my advice.

'Listen to me rabbiting on. You are listening though aren't you? I mean, you're not thinking about trains or something are you?'

Spencer shakes his head. He was thinking about trains for a bit, but not anymore. He likes listening to Goldy, and watching all her expressions—he's never known anyone with so many expressions and gestures.

'So, one day, this man came into this restaurant I was working in, and it was quite classy, with a passable wine list. I think I'd just turned nineteen. He was having dinner with his wife, and he asked for a bottle of the Châteauneuf-du-Pape—I can remember it like it was yesterday—and I told him it wasn't a patch on the Saint-Émilion Grand Cru, and that's ten pounds less. He took his glasses off and narrowed his eyes at me. I thought he was about to cause a scene. But no, he asked me about the other wines, and he offered me a job there and then—as a sommelier in his own restaurant. Do you know what that is Spencer?'

'Yes Goldy. It's French for a wine waiter.'

'You're not as daft as you look,' she says, shoving his elbow off his knee.

Spontaneously, Spencer's mouth turns up at the corners.

'It just so happened to be a top restaurant in Soho, and I moved to London, which was amazing, and I made loads of friends. Again, I gained a reputation, and before I knew it, I had this job working for Majestic, jetting all over the world, and choosing wine. It was my dream job, I loved every minute of it. You see, not only was I choosing wine and visiting all these exotic places, I was also being treated like royalty by vineyard owners who were trying to sell me their produce. All men of course, and most of them thought I was just a silly, little girl who didn't know a Chardonnay from a Sauvignon Blanc. Most of them were schmoozers. I would be picked up at the airport, taken out for dinner, lavished with gifts—the works—and all because I was a buyer for this massive company, and they thought I was a pushover. What they didn't realize was I took wine far too seriously to be bought or charmed.'

She prods the fire and they both watch the sparks fly.

'Six months it lasted. I was at this vineyard in Chile. Beautiful it was—snow-capped mountains looming in the background. The man who ran it was American and he was very charismatic, but a little overbearing and full of himself. I was confident myself, didn't take any crap, and thought I knew everything. But I was naïve you see, still green about the gills, and thought nothing bad would happen to me.' She sighs. 'Well, you know where this is going, don't you?'

Spencer doesn't know, and he's frowning hard to make it come sooner.

'Well, he persuaded me to stay in his ranch didn't he? Great big place it was. It's just the two of us, it's romantic... the heat, the mountains, the wine—don't forget the wine— we drank a lot of wine...'

She's playing with the fire again, but looking beyond it.

'He flirted with me, made me laugh, told me I was beautiful; and it was nice, and I warmed to him, and he seemed like a gentleman... He was anything but, and, very, very quickly, things turned ugly.' She fixes him with a stare. 'Do you know what rape is Spencer?'

After holding her stare for a moment, he looks down and shakes his head slowly.

'You're lucky. You don't need to know, and I wish I didn't either.' She sighs, and Spencer does the same. 'Well, that was it. Game over. I lost my confidence overnight. I couldn't tell anyone about it, became ill, just wanted to be on my own, and retreated deeper and deeper into depression... drink...

drugs... Within a month I was homeless. I'd fallen to pieces and I was just twenty.'

Spencer's still listening, listening with all his might, but he's a bit confused.

'You know that phone call I had the other day? Well, that was my counsellor. I'm still fucked up Spencer. Do you understand?'

Spencer doesn't know what to say, or even what Goldy wants him to say, so he doesn't say anything.

'A few months after the... after Chile... I pulled myself together... Well, a little, but I wasn't able to work, or become a member of society again. I've been on the dole and mostly living in squats ever since. Things can never be the same again.'

'It's like the corpuscles, Goldy.'

'Yes, like the corpuscles, Spencer. I became dependent on alcohol... drugs... you name it. Well, I've been clean for five years. The last squat was supposed to be clean as well, but it's impossible to keep a squat clean, not with those people. All squatters have been raped; literally, or by life. In my case it was literally, and I've never had anything to do with men since. So, that was why I moved here. You're going to tell me you're an alcoholic now aren't you?'

Spencer's jaw drops. 'No... I don't drink. I'm like you. Goldy.'

'I was pulling your leg.'

'Pulling my leg, yes... Mum's an alcoholic, and I think she might be homeless again.'

'Oh dear, sorry to hear that.' Goldy notices the time on Spencer's watch. 'That reminds me, I'm supposed to see *my* mum today. She's a responsible drinker, just in case you were wondering. But I'll ask you about *your* mum next time OK? Don't tell her about this place though, because this house is clean, and I'm going to put a sign on the door.'

She gets up and a shaft of light turns her hair to spun gold, like the straw in *Rumpelstiltskin*.

'You said I had to ask you another question,' Spencer says, ashen in the shadows.

'So I did. Well, I have to honour a promise, don't I? What is it then?'

She remains standing, and Spencer watches gold flecks of dust above her head.

'Would you like to go on a steam train with me?'

She laughs so loud and so long it seems the whole room is laughing along with her—the walls, the grandfather clock, the bookcases—the lot. Goldy leans over Spencer and hugs his head to her.

'You should be on the National Health. Now, I really must fly.'

She's still giggling when she's come back downstairs.

'One day Spencer, I will shave my legs and put on a posh frock, and we will go on one of your blessed steam trains— and that's a promise.'

Later, when Spencer leaves, and he glances back from the poplars, the house looks a little bit happy and a little bit sad; and tramping up the track, the same frogs from yesterday are hellbent on getting past him, and the dragonflies flick him with their wings.

He tries to picture the vineyard in Chile with the snow-capped mountains, which is where she soared away from him. He couldn't follow her, because her tale was all about people forging closeness, and he's heard so many tales like this before, and been left for dust every time.

When the bus is nearing the estate, and he has to pay attention, he realizes the rest of the journey was a blur, and he didn't even notice the make or model. He's been thinking about Goldy, and not about her job, or going to Chile, or any of that. No, he's been thinking about her corpuscles, and seeing them ebbing and flowing along rivers in her body, silhouetted against the sun, and the corpuscles are golden pastilles, and the rivers, white tubes. It's not just her either; it's the house, all the plants around it and the earth it sits on—all of them are flat against the sun, and all of them have tubes of golden pastilles flowing through them, and out of and into each other; they're all connected, they're all one.

When the doors open, and he says, thank you driver, he can still see corpuscles in the road, in the path to E block, inside E block, and in the teenagers hidden somewhere, except all of them are black. Now he comes to think of it, he can't imagine the teenagers doing normal things, like having a bowl of Rice Krispies or going to the toilet. It's as if they're not real people at all, but made of paper and go to sleep in between books in bookcases, or turn to piles of sand when no one's looking and return to the walls.

The bus shelter separates him, a shield, that's something, and he waits there, his legs barely supporting him.

Two hours and six minutes he waits, unable to proceed, and then he sees someone he knows from his floor who he could accompany on the path and in the lift, and it's Mr Macready from 1911. Customary blue plastic bag clinking, he's unsteady on his feet, slaloming down the road; a good excuse for Spencer to say hello and take him by the arm, and a kindness he's only too happy to accept. Spencer's eyes wide and darting, it takes a while to negotiate bins, walls and doors, but once inside the building they only need await the lift. There's no one in the lobby, and once summoned, while his eyes flit between the main doors and flashing numbers, every clunk of the lift's torturous descent is met with a flinch. Once inside the cage, and Spencer's selected nineteen, and he's pressing the 'close doors' button on repeat, still they won't close. Someone's approaching, and still they won't close, and there's no escape, and Mr Macready wouldn't be able to protect him, probably wouldn't even notice, and the animal is somersaulting. It's a burka with a pram, and taking in the lurching figure, the reek of booze and urine, she speaks crossly in her language and reverses. And, even as the lift doors trundle along their tracks, they could come bundling in, and he'd be trapped, and they'd cut him down, and the blood would spill over the floor and down the gap in the doorway into the shaft, and spread out thinly from the never-ending shuntings, and some of his corpuscles would remain forever. But they don't come in, not even when there's an inch of space, and their hands could still prise the doors open, and he's seen it so many times in films, even then it doesn't happen, and, when the cage jerks back to life, they both collapse in a huddle. They're safe now, because after the ground floor no one gets in when it's going up, and as they lie there, pinned down by gravity, they breathe easy.

Snowdrop is there to greet him, rubbing herself against any part she can reach; and attempting to meld her scent with these strange smells of burning and wildness, she searches his eyes for further clues on his adventuring. Apart from her attentions, continuing long after she's been fed, the rooms he wanders through aimlessly are steeped in sadness, and not so much unfriendly, as indifferent. It's as if the furniture, and even the walls, and his possessions, feel betrayed.

Noticing the flashing, red 'one' on his ansaphone, he plays back the message while Snowdrop nuzzles his face and purrs loudly.

'I've just been evicted thanks to you. Are you happy now?'

'What about borrowing some money off him? Did you try that?' another drunken voice can be heard saying.

'I wouldn't borrow a penny off that bastard if he was the last person on Earth. Forty-eight hours I was in labour with him, and this is how he repays me. He's no son of mine. I disown him.'

The line goes dead.

'End of messages.'

15

It's two days later and Spencer is waking up. The problem is it's not his bed, and neither is it Goldy's sofa. He has no idea where he is, how he came to be here, and whose pyjamas he's wearing. Another conundrum is his head hurts, and feeling it, he discovers a bandage. He'd like to get out of this bed and find out what's behind the blue curtain that goes around the bed on three sides, and it can't be a window, unless, that is, he's in a greenhouse or a submarine conning tower. It's a long way down to the floor, and a further conundrum is posed by the tube attached to his arm with sticky tape, which could be attached with a needle, and he hates needles, and can't even look, and just the thought of it makes him feel sick and his head spin. The smell reminds him of Sunrise and so do the murmuring voices, and he wonders if he's been kidnapped and taken back there without his knowledge, and knocked out, and that's why he can't remember anything and his head hurts.

Presently, a nurse comes in through an opening in the curtain, and tells him to remain calm, he's in the Princess Royal, where he was admitted after sustaining a head injury. That's all she knows, because she's just come on shift, and doing a ward round, and the doctor will be in soon. She takes the tube out and assists him to the toilet, when he discovers he's in pain all over, and hardly recognizes himself in the mirror underneath all the bruising. When he's back in bed, the nurse puts the tube back in. The whole time he feels sick and his head spins.

The nurse's information has calmed him down a fraction, and wiggling his toes from left to right over and over again, a fraction more.

'Spencer Morton?' asks a man with a clipboard, who says he's a doctor with an unpronounceable name, after breakfast has been served on a plastic tray that looks like wood.

The doctor explains he'd been found unconscious at six a.m. yesterday on the stairwell of a block of flats, and when coming round he was in a state of shock. Investigations showed contusions to the head, arms and legs, consistent with a fall, but due to his unwillingness to cooperate, he'd been sedated so they could do tests and x-rays, the results of which don't point at lasting damage to the cerebral cortex, only that he's suffering from post-traumatic stress. When admitted to a ward for observation, he became highly agitated to the point he had to be restrained and sedated again, and slept for the remainder of the day and the following night.

Spencer takes very little of this in, partly because he's trying to remember what he was doing on the stairwell at six-hundred hours, and also because the unpronounceable doctor's tie is the same shade of blue as the curtain and looks like a hole in his chest.

'Now then, Spencer... You don't mind if I call you Spencer?... Now then, Spencer, someone from where you ive has been in touch with your social worker, who I'm quite sure will visit you soon enough. Is there anyone else we can call for you?... Anyone at all?... Someone who lives with you?... Parent or guardian?... Brother? Sister? Friend? Neighbour? Anyone at all?'

Spencer doesn't say a word, shake his head or make any other perceptible movement.

'Well, I'm sure your... er... your social worker will be in very soon. If there's-'

'Snowdrop will starve to death,' Spencer says, trying to get out of bed until a stabbing pain in his arm reminds him what's attached to it.

'Snowdrop being your cat?...' the doctor says, restraining him gently. 'Is there no one who has a key to your property, who could look after him or her?'

'She'll starve to death, she'll starve to death, she'll starve to death.'

Spencer is sedated again.

The next thing he's aware of is a man with a flowery shirt and round, stripy-framed glasses sitting on his bed alongside a box of stuffed animals.

'Are there any you'd like to hold? Lots of patients find that cuddling a soft toy makes them feel better. Go on, take your pick—they won't bite. How about Kenneth the Koala?'

Robert comes in later.

'My God! Look at the state of you.'

He takes an array of forms out of his canvas shoulder-bag, strewing them over the bed before flopping in the chair with a sigh.

'Honestly Spencer,' he hisses, 'have you any idea how much work you give me? If you're not making a nuisance of yourself on steam trains or getting lost on buses, you're getting into scrapes with teenagers. And now this! I ask you... I've got to fill out a C-three, a C-four *and* a D-two! I'll need to have a meeting with my supervisor, consider the health and safety implications... Honestly, you have no idea... And quite how I'm supposed to concentrate with Big Bird eyeballing me, heaven only knows.' He shoves the offending three-foot creature off the bed, where it's out of view, except for one orange leg sticking straight up.

'So, I've spoken to building security and they gave me the gen. Do you remember anything, Spencer?'

Silence.

Robert's phone bleeps.

'What's the last thing you remember?'

Silence.

Robert's phone bleeps.

'All I can tell you is the security guard's account. I wrote it down somewhere...' Wading through his shoulder-bag, and retrieving a spiralbound pad, he flicks through it. 'Ah, here we are... *Found unconscious May fourteen at six a.m.* Why were you out at that time Spencer?... *Seventh floor landing...* Why didn't you use the lift?' Robert no longer looks at Spencer, and talks to himself. '*Ronald Higgins, apartment 504...* Who's he?... Oh, I see—he discovered you. Can't read my own writing... Wait a minute... If he lives on the fifth floor... what was he doing on the seventh floor?.. This is a case for Poirot, not an overloaded social worker. Where did I get to?... *Taken to Princess Royal A&E by ambulance. Woke in a distressed state, suffering from trauma, shouting, incoherent, unable or unwilling to answer questions-* That's my Spencer... You know who your worst enemy is? It's not Ryan Henderson, it's you. Yes, *you* Spencer. You're always getting into trouble. *You*, Spencer. What were you doing on the stairs at six a.m.? The doctors were only trying to help you, and you clam up—just like you're doing now... Let's see... *Had to be sedated. Bruising to head, face, limbs. Initial tests revealed no serious damage to brain function... Taken to ward nine for observation. Became delirious, endlessly chanting train statistics-* That's my Spencer... *Required further sedation...* and on the way in, the doctor informed me you slept soundly until seven this morning.

'Well, that's about the size of it Spencer.' Robert returns the pad to his shoulder-bag, takes his glasses off and rubs his eyes. 'Now, please try to cast your mind back. Do you have any memory of leaving your flat yesterday at six a.m. via the stairwell?'

Silence.

'Spencer, *please-*'

Robert's phone bleeps. He takes it out, looks at it and puts it back in his pocket.

'Snowdrop will starve to death.' Spencer tries to get out of bed.

'You're not going anywhere.' Robert pins him down.

'She'll starve to death, she'll starve-'

'She won't starve to death Spencer.' Then mutters under his breath, 'It's only a cat for Christ's sake.'

'She'll starve to death, she'll-'

'Spencer!'

'Who will starve to death?' A nurse pops through the opening.

'It's alright thank you nurse—he's talking about a cat. Alright Spencer, I'll see what I can do. Don't worry about it.'

The nurse smiles at Spencer and disappears.

'Listen, I'll grab a coffee and get started on the paper-work.' Robert picks up the forms from the bed. 'Meanwhile, you take it easy, don't get yourself worked up—but see if you can recollect something from the events prior to your fall.'

When he comes back, Spencer has calmed down, and says he doesn't remember anything. Robert finishes off the paperwork, with which Spencer helps as much as he's able, mainly nodding and shaking his head.

'I'll have to leave you now,' Robert says later, 'I've had to reschedule two meetings as it is. The doctor told me you're going to be transferred to another ward because this one's short-term, and they want to keep you in for observation-Don't get anxious Spencer, it's just a precaution. Meanwhile, I'll let your job coach know what's happened, she'll contact your employment liaison officer, who will let your workplace know you won't be coming in for-The doctor says you can't go back to work yet Spencer, that's just the way it is.

'When you're better I think we might need to call a case review to look at your long-term future. It could be that your needs will be better met by returning to supported accom-modation.'

Spencer's eyes are open wide.

'I'll see what can be done about your cat…' Muttering as he stands up, 'As if I don't have enough to do… I'll be back to see you when I can find the time—Oh, and I'll let Mrs Adeoye know about the accident as well.'

Because there's no other beds available, Spencer's trans-ferred to a children's ward, which has Lego, and he finds that building models, taking them apart and rebuilding them, helps to pass the time.

Mostly though, he's keeping quiet, rocking back and forth, and thinking about Snowdrop, Goldy and Goldy's house. He doesn't even have her number. Neither does he have Mrs Jenkins or any other neighbours' numbers, which would be helpful in a situation like this. He's never been in a situation like this though, that's the thing. Mrs Jenkins has a spare set of keys, and she's fed Snowdrop before, but without her number that's not much use. His mother said she could keep a spare set for him, but when he'd told her Robert wouldn't let her, she'd flown into one of her rages, when there's no talking to her, and she stormed out.

He stays in the children's ward for a couple of weeks, which is alright, because, as well as Lego, there are lots of entertainers and activities, and he likes children's telly, children's films and children's food.

One day Mrs Adeoye comes in, and everyone stares because of her uniform and handcuffs swinging on her belt, and Desmond, who's another special needs, takes her baton off her, which wouldn't be difficult because of the size of her tummy, and runs up and down the ward hitting other children with it. When she's got it back, she explains to the senior nurse she doesn't have the right forms with her to take matters further, and it's up to the hospital or the parents if they want to press charges. Muttering about not being paid enough for this crap, she draws the curtains around Spencer's bed, which have characters from *Frozen* on them, and they're on the walls, balls, toys, plates, cups, dressing-up outfits and the baseball caps the nurses wear.

Just like Robert, Mrs Adeoye has a lot of paperwork to go

through, and she also spreads it over the bed, and Spencer has to sit on the pillow clasping his knees tightly so he doesn't crumple the forms, and every now and then she pushes his foot back. Intermittently, crackling and unintelligible speech come out of her walkie-talkie, and she keeps needing help with spelling, and although Spencer knows how to spell every word, she goes off to find a nurse each time.

When questioned repeatedly, Spencer still doesn't remember anything about the fall, or even what he was doing on the stairs at that time, and Mrs Adeoye says he's not being much help. She says she'll check the CCTV, but doesn't hold out much hope. This reminds her there's no CCTV footage for the incident behind the car park, because the cameras weren't working. However, she's spoken to Ryan Henderson and some other teenagers, and warned them to keep away from him. Spencer goes very quiet at this point, the animal wakes up, and he doesn't say anything, and tries to picture Goldy's finger tattoos and the shapes on the rug.

'I've got another matter to discuss with you,' Mrs Adeoye says, putting one file away and bringing out another. 'I'm not best pleased with it to be honest. CID should be dealing with it, but it's been dumped on muggins here, because you're special needs.'

Spencer isn't listening. He's got enough on his plate, what with worrying about Snowdrop, the caged animal's antics, and trying to calm it down by picturing Goldy and her house.

'So, I'm required by law to read the transcript out to you, or at least the bit that's about you- You're not being arrested, or anything like that. Well, I couldn't arrest you, not without a parent or guardian, or social worker, or someone like that.

I've sent a copy to Robert, and I'm leaving a copy with you... Where did I leave yours... So many bits of paper—drives you round the bend. Ah, here it is. Here... Take it then. Now I've got to tick this box, and enter the date and time in these boxes, to say it's in your possession.'

Spencer watches her do these things, and read out each word and number aloud, and rocks back and forth as far as his constricted position allows.

'Can you write your name, luv?' She hands him the pen. 'Your initials... an X... Oh, you can do it. Let me see if I can read it... Yes, very good. You need to write the date and time—Oh, you've done it already. That was quick. Let me check to see if you got it right.'

While this is going on, Spencer has already read the paragraph upside-down that she's highlighted in yellow and ringed with red asterisks. The animal is throwing itself against the cage. Repeatedly. Goldy's not there and neither is her house. There's only blackness and spinning.

'So, yes, as I was saying, you can ask someone else to read it for you and explain it in simple words. But, yes, I have to read out this bit to you.' She clears her throat, underlining the gravity of the situation. '*When asked how they had found out when the whisky delivery would be, two of the three suspects (Kozlowski and Briggs) quoted "Spencer Morton", a shelf-stacker at the afore-mentioned store, as being the source. He informed them when it would arrive, the vehicle's registration, the probable route, the name of the driver, that he always used the toilet at the store and bought a chilled can of Red Bull. He also knew how many cases were to be delivered, and the total quantity in the vehicle. Briggs added that, although Morton is, in his words, "a mental case"' he's "obsessed with facts and figures", aided by "a photographic memory". Kozlowski added, that Morton is, in his words, "spastyczny". Both suspects explained Morton had provided the information with the understanding he was to receive a case of Whyte and Mackay.'*

Returning her copy of the printout to a transparent document wallet, Mrs Adeoye signs and dates a box on her checklist, and somehow, through the spinning void, Spencer follows suit.

After she's gone, he continues to rock silently in the same constricted space, as if Mrs Adeoye's hand created a force field.

He's moulded something out of the darkness though, and instead of everything spinning about him, and applying centrifugal force to his tummy, he's been able to put it on the outside, where it rotates in a vortex, like the one in the opening sequence of *Doctor Who* in the old days, and it feels quite nice, and safe, because no one can get to him in there.

Later, much later, when he's lying in bed, it's dark and quiet, and he can only make out the *Frozen* characters by their shapes, the house comes back to him. Not only that, because soon it's so vivid, he feels he's there in the living room, and if he pulled back the curtain there would be hundreds of candle pots, and each with hundreds of points of light. He can see the fire, and hear its contented crackles. He can see the glow of the fire on one side of Goldy's face too, and in her eyes, and on her teeth— because she's smiling at him, and it feels as though her smile will never fade. She's pulling him, that's what it feels like. Or rather, *they're* pulling him—Goldy, the house, and all the plants, and the trees and the earth surrounding them. He can see them all; and the grass, the trees are leaning towards him, and even the house ever so slightly. They're all one, and their corpuscles are all on one side, the side closest to him, and they're dragging his corpuscles towards them. His corpuscles are golden pastilles just like theirs, and they want to ebb and flow with the others, because they should be together, they should be one.

16

It's two weeks later, Spencer's bandage has been taken off, he's waking up, and he's in his own bed at long last. He could have woken up in his bed a week ago, but he had to wait for Robert to escort him because the hospital wouldn't let him leave on his own, and he didn't have his independent travel certificate with him. The doctor with the unpronounceable name told him they needed the bed, and it wasn't a hotel, and kept leaving messages on Robert's phone, but he didn't get back to them.

When Robert came in, Spencer heard him talking to the doctor about having problems with picking up messages, and this was yet another glitch with his phone, after a string of them, and he would like to change his provider, but it was a work phone and outside his control. He also heard Robert saying he'd given a nurse contact details of family members who could escort him when he last came in, but he didn't know her name and couldn't point her out or describe her, and there the trail went cold. Spencer wondered which family members Robert was talking about, because he couldn't think of any who would do something like that, or even that it had anything to do with them.

Robert drove Spencer in his mustard one-litre, three-cylinder Fiat five-hundred, fitted with a child-lock as standard, which Robert always uses when Spencer's in the car. During the journey he discussed the whisky heist, as he called it. How could Spencer be so naïve as to provide all this information about the delivery? Didn't he think it was suspicious that these individuals wanted to know all these details about the lorry, whether the driver went to the toilet, picked his nose or had hairy knuckles? Well, he had said, shunting between stationary vehicles on the dual carriageway, Spencer would just have to wait and see if he was called before a court of law, and Robert wouldn't be able to help him then, because it would be outside his remit. He went on to say he couldn't believe that one person could get in so much trouble, it was just one thing after another, and he would end up in prison at this rate, even before a review could be called to determine if he'd be safer in supported accommodation, which would be ironic given prison is exactly that.

Spencer wasn't listening, or at least trying very hard not to, because it churned up his tummy. Instead, he thought about his corpuscles, and how, with every twist, turn and undulation in the road, they shifted round a bit to face the house, and he realized why he saw them as pastilles, and it was because of the word, and rather than corpuscles and blood—which make him feel sick—he saw them as 'core pastilles' flowing along white rivers and lit up gold by the sun.

Robert wanted to leave him at the main doors, but Spencer begged him to come up in the lift. Spencer invited him in for a cup of tea with protocol biscuits, but he said he had an appointment, and couldn't see Spencer to his door, and remained in the lift.

As soon as he unlocked the door Spencer knew something was wrong, because Snowdrop didn't come to greet him. He knew she'd be under the bed, where she was still and silent in the corner, with scared eyes. Spencer had to put her food under the bed, and talk to her, and make comforting sounds, and when she still wouldn't budge, he had to leave her alone in the hope she'd venture out. When eventually she ate her food and drank some water, she paced up and down the hall and whined pitifully, and when Spencer tried to stroke her, she ran under the bed every time. She looked even thinner than she usually did, shivering and wobbling with every step, and her lovely white coat had lost its shine.

He can't believe she hasn't been fed in all this time—or rather, *won't* believe it—and thinks he's been away four weeks. It's not so much that she's still alive after all this time that amazes him, it's more that Rob- no, he won't think about it, and decides that someone *has* been putting out food for her, but she hasn't been eating it out of concern for Spencer. The two of them have been worried sick for each other the whole time.

At least she had access to water, because he'd left the bathroom door wedged open, and he's seen her drink out of the toilet before.

There were eleven messages on his ansaphone, all from Mum, and she sounded drunk in every single one, not that he listened to them, and deleted them one by one as soon as he knew it was her.

Spencer has an appointment with his GP later, and Mrs Jenkins goes with him in the lift, and waits for him to come back, so they can go up together, and he buys her a tin of throat pastilles in the chemist's (where he picks up a prescription for more blue pills) because she coughs a lot, and they're red, not gold. Robert told him to go to the health centre for a sick note, and post it to his workplace, because the doctor in the hospital said he was to rest and recuperate for another two weeks.

Mrs Jenkins' son, Thomas, has gone back to his wife to try and patch things up because life's not worth living without her. This means Spencer and Mrs Jenkins will have to escort each other in the lift, and Spencer's drawn up two timetables for the next seven days, which are identical: one for him and one for her, and they have the times when they will be going out, so the other one knows. Spencer doesn't have anywhere to go, apart from one shopping trip, but he's put down that he will go for a walk each day at fourteen-hundred hours, which his GP said is good for the constitution, as long as he doesn't overexert himself. Mrs Jenkins has a lot of appointments and classes at the day centre, which is a different one to the one Spencer goes to, because it's for normal old people and not adults with special needs—including old people with special needs—and Spencer doesn't think he can go there because neither is he normal nor old. Mrs Jenkins says there will be times when something crops up or one of them runs out of milk, that kind of thing, and then they will have to wing it and be flexible. Spencer's not very happy about winging it, or being flexible, and would rather know in advance when things are going to happen, and stick to the timetable, but says he will try his hardest.

The only trouble is returning, unless the one who does the escorting doesn't mind waiting in the vestibule until the other one gets back. Mrs Jenkins doesn't mind because there are seats down there, and she can take her knitting. Spencer does mind though, he minds a lot, which means Mrs Jenkins has to wait until someone else from their floor comes in. This still doesn't resolve the problem of Spencer taking Mrs Jenkins down, and being left alone when she goes off. During these times he goes outside, where he thinks he could get away from the teenagers more easily, instead of being cornered in the vestibule. He stays close to the building, where there's always men hanging about and waiting in cars, and he thinks the teenagers wouldn't attack him in front of them, but he still keeps his eyes and ears open. It's not so bad for Spencer though, because he's decided that anyone on the top three floors is an acceptable escort, which is fifty-seven apartments, and he recognizes all of these people, as well as some of the nurses and carers who visit them, and it never takes more than a few minutes for one of them to come in, and he can run up the last couple of flights. He always asks them if they don't mind going up with him, and none of them do, and even the ones who can't speak English nod and smile, unless they wear burkas and then they just nod. Mrs Jenkins can't do this because of her arthritis, and has to wait for someone from the nineteenth floor.

When they use the lift together, Spencer's more anxious than she is—even though he takes a pill an hour before they're due to go down—and every time the lift stops to pick up other people, which it always does, he moves closer and holds her hand. He's so worried about the teenagers coming in, that's the thing, and in the lift there's no escape, and if

Mrs Jenkins has a heart attack or faints, they could attack him without her even knowing.

Now that he's back in 1919, he's been thinking about the teenagers a lot. When he was in hospital he didn't have to think about them, and could stop himself, and make everything go black, or think about nice things, like Goldy or trains. He still can't remember why he was on the stairs at six-hundred hours on May the fourteenth, let alone what caused him to fall, whether he was coming or going, or anything, and now it's June the twelfth. It wasn't a work day, as he wasn't due back at work until the fifteenth, and anyway, he doesn't get back until eight-hundred hours at the earliest. Because he can't think of any other reason as to where he was going at that time, and how he fell, he thinks it must be in some way connected to the teenagers, and maybe they have special powers, or at least the one with the freckles, and he looks like the kind of person who would have them. Maybe they're shapeshifters who live in the walls, and they can appear anytime in any part of the building, and drip out of the concrete in liquid form and then solidify. But then they could drip into 1919, and he'd rather not think of that possibility.

He's frightened, that's the main thing, very, very frightened. The one with the freckles said he would cut him from mouth to ear if he went to the police again, and he *did* go to the police (or rather, the police came to him) and the teenagers know all about it, because Mrs Adeoye has warned them to stay away from him. If it *was* them though, and they attacked him, and pushed him down the stairs, why didn't they kill him? It would have been quiet on the stairs at that time and he was out cold, and they could have taken their time to cut him exactly how they wanted.

Anyway, the main thing is, sooner or later they're going to get him, that's all there is to it, unless, that is, he kills himself or runs away. He's not going to do either of these things, but he is going to see Goldy, he's going to her house tomorrow, and he's going to tell her everything and ask for her help.

17

It's 05.17 the next day and Spencer's on his way to Goldy's house. He wanted to leave early, as soon as it was light. He hasn't got very far yet, only the stairwell on the eighteenth floor. The thing is, because he's so frightened of falling—especially when his legs are like jelly—he's shuffling down on his bottom. The first time he left, and started shuffling, he thought his bottom might get sore after four-hundred-and-fifty-six stairs, which is the total number, and after one flight he went back for a cushion. He's got his yellow backpack rather than the orange rucksack, as it's easier to carry the smaller one going down the stairs like this, and he's holding it in his lap. He's sorry to leave Snowdrop so soon after her ordeal, and she hasn't calmed down yet, still won't let him stroke her and wouldn't sleep on the bed for the second night in a row. He thinks he should take her to the vet's in case there's something wrong with her, but he can't risk it in case he sees the teenagers, and he wouldn't be able to run very fast with the pet carrier, and they might take her off him, and cut her as well as him, and he would never forgive himself.

It takes forty-seven minutes to go all the way down, and

he becomes more and more agitated with each floor (even though he took two blue pills last night, and two when he got up) and to be absolutely certain no one's coming, the pauses between each stair grow longer. The trouble is, due to his level of agitation and fright, it feels like the animal is punching his eardrums, he has to strain harder to listen, and now his ears hurt. No one does come of course, not at this time, and it's deserted outside, when he gets up and walks normally, or as normal as his jellified legs allow.

He has to wait until 06.41 for the number 37, which is less frequent at this time of day, but that's alright, because it's a main road, someone else is waiting there, and he feels safe.

Soon after he gets on the bus, which is the B7TL again, and sits on the left-hand side of the back seat on the lower deck (his favourite position) two teenagers get on and sit in front of him. He didn't see their faces, and they have their hoods up, but he knows they're teenagers from the way they talk and fidget. Teenagers are always fidgeting, and making sudden, fast movements, and you never know what they're going to do next.

He's not trying to listen to their conversation or anything, but it's quiet on the bus, and he hears anyway.

'He says I can borrow it,' the one on the left says. 'You should see it. Tight. Not as heavy as I thought—solid—good to hold 'n shit.'

'Whadja wanna do with it bro'?' the other one asks.

'I just wanna… you know… see what it feels like.'

'Yeah, but what on? Rats 'n shit?'

'Nah, rats is for kids innit? I wanna waste someone.'

'Yeah, but you'll do time for that bro'.'

'Not if I don't get caught,' the one on the left says with a chuckle, and his shoulders go up and down.

'Whodja wanna waste bro?' asks the other one, his shoulders going up and down too. 'Yer old man?'

'Nah, no one like that. I'm talkin' about a mong, or a druggie… or… or an old cunt. 'Coz then I'll know what it's like to waste someone real.'

They go on like this for a while, and Spencer doesn't know what they're talking about, and maybe it's a computer game or a film. They get off in the city centre, along with everyone else—everyone except Spencer—because he's going right through, out the other side and into the countryside, and his core pastilles are all at the front of his body and face, and the core pastilles of Goldy, the house and the nature around it are all leaning towards him.

June is well-advanced, and the banks are swollen with new additions: cornflowers, devil's-bit scabious, lush swathes of yarrow, and poppies throughout, like beads of blood. The corn is higher, gold-tipped and rolling in the moist air. This time it's the turn of seed spores, floating in the honeyed breeze, to point the way for the hapless adventurer, caressing him by and by. The mighty poplars are in full leaf, and they are happy, as all living things should be when days are long and juices flowing. The house is happy too, because the visitor has come back, and the custodian is there, sitting in the garden, where Spencer sees her from a distance, steam rising from her coffee, bees buzzing overhead like acolytes, her hair a golden halo. And all the core pastilles are happy, and can ebb and flow within themselves and between each other once more, and mingle and join forces, and draw strength from one another.

'Well, well, well,' Goldy says, looking up upon hearing rustlings in the undergrowth. 'Ooh! What's happened to your face?' Coffee sloshes in her mug as she rises.

'I had an accident Goldy,' he says, as he sits down on the bench and she follows suit, 'I fell down the stairs in E block at six-hundred hours on May the fourteenth and Mr Higgins from 504 found me unconscious.'

'That's terrible,' she says stroking his shoulder. 'What were you doing out at that time?'

'I don't remember anything; not getting up, or anything at all. But I suspect foul play,' he says, nodding gravely.

'Foul play? How do you mean?'

And he goes on to tell her all about the teenagers, and all the things they've done to him, and how he's terrified to go in and out of the building on his own, and he tells her all about his time in hospital as well, how Snowdrop's painfully thin, he's on pills for his anxiety, and he still hasn't got his X-wing back.

And Goldy listens intently, asks questions, and wears a concerned expression as she looks down (because she's taller than him) and her brow is furrowed, and she looks into his eyes, and strokes his shoulder, hands and hair.

She makes another coffee, and two bacon sandwiches, and camomile tea, telling him it has calming properties. They sit on the bench again because it's nice out, much nicer than being inside she says, and she sits outside a lot in the daytime. Birds are singing, bees are buzzing, crickets are chirruping, and all in all it couldn't be lovelier.

'Would you like me to dig up the garden for you Goldy?'

'Er…' She looks around, as if confused by the question.

'I learned digging at Sunrise and I've got a gardening certificate. I could dig up all the weeds and-'

'There's no such thing as weeds Spencer, only plants, and all plants are equal, just like all people are equal.'

Spencer doesn't know what to say to this; he's like a motor that won't start. 'Well... I... I could... How... What... I could tidy it up a bit, and I could plant some seeds, and you wouldn't need to do anything, and I would do everything.'

'I like it messy though, wild and messy, just like me.'

'But... but... but...' Spencer's never heard the like.

Goldy puts a finger to his lips and takes him by the hand towards the house, and he falters and stumbles, but she's bold and sure-footed for the two of them.

'What do you think of my sign?' she asks, referring to the piece of cardboard tacked on the inner door, saying, 'no drugs, no drink'.

'I've never had drugs or alcohol in my life Goldy and I don't tell lies. Dad died from an overdose and Mum's an alcoholic.'

'You're such a literalist,' she says, as they put the dishes in the washing-up tub. 'It's a statement of intent, and, well, a way to remind myself this is a special place, and it mustn't be spoiled. Do you understand?'

Spencer does understand, and anyway, he's powerless when she fixes him with one of those stares.

Goldy says she's going to boil some water to wash herself and the dishes, she's got to make some phone calls, and then they'll have lunch.

Spencer sits outside and waits.

'You know it's not your fault your mum's an alcoholic

don't you?' Goldy says when they're sitting on the bench again, having finished lunch.

Spencer doesn't know, but he nods all the same, and he watches her fingers idly picking gooseberries off a bush.

'I have previous, and been in counselling for years, and counselled other people, so I'm a bit of an authority on the subject.'

The berries are impossibly round and golden in the hazy sunshine; but they're not ripe, and biting into one with her strong white teeth, it's expelled with force.

'I was drinking myself to death, and no one could stop me except myself. I'm sure you and countless other people have tried to help your mum, but if she decides to keep on drinking, there's nothing anyone else can do about it. I've helped loads of people, but I don't have *anything* to do with those who are still abusing.'

Spencer notices how she spits the word 'anything' out, and the gooseberries tremble on their stalks.

'You can't make any headway with an alcoholic until they've stopped drinking, it's as simple as that; and neither can you make any headway unless an alcoholic is *entirely* honest with you and themselves.'

Fixing him with a stare, he trembles too.

'I've stopped drinking. I stopped five years ago, haven't touched it since; and I'm entirely honest with myself and everyone else—but I'm still an alcoholic and always will be.'

Spencer's eyes grow big.

Goldy laughs. 'You have no idea how cute you look when you pull that face.'

Later, when they're having home-made soup in front of the fire, Spencer remembers the printout, and shows it to her, and she reads it as the flames leap up, and he watches her face, and how she licks her fingers and makes little smacking sounds. Occasionally she chuckles. With midsummer fast approaching, the light is strong enough at this time of day to probe the inner reaches and pick out dancing specks of dust. A few candles have been lit, and together, their sparkles, the softer sunbeams, and the interplay between them and the glowing hearth—much like the core pastilles—have fashioned an enchanted grotto.

'My goodness, you lead an exciting life,' she says, when she's got through all the pages. 'If you're not evading the clutches of marauding, knife-wielding teenagers and a half-cut, violent mother, or falling down stairs in the early hours, you're mixing with gangsters and wanted by the cops as an informant. My little life holed up in a country house is dull as ditch-water by comparison. I think I might need to come to the city to live it up for a bit. How do you fancy a sidekick?... Spencer and Goldy... doesn't quite have the ring of Bonnie and Clyde does it? Not that I could be involved in stealing hard liquor of course. Now, if it was a Terry's All Gold lorry,' she says, reaching for the box Spencer gave her today, 'that would be a different matter.'

Spencer's never thought about people eating before, how it can look so nice. He hasn't followed most of what she's said, but he still likes listening to her voice, the words she uses, how her face moves, and well, everything really. He takes a chocolate too, when they're offered, except he knows the way he eats is ordinary.

'Not exactly criminal masterminds are they, your associates.' She hands him the pages. 'I know, let's hijack a whisky lorry, with a cargo worth... What did it say?' She takes the

ADRIAN KEEFE

pages back. 'Fifty-eight-thousand pounds. But, then, let's pull over round the corner, down a bottle between us, and then carry on driving, and who cares if we crash into a tree we're too plastered to run, and we're caught red-handed. Sounds great! What are we waiting for?'

Spencer doesn't want to hijack a lorry, or any of those things she mentioned. He can't drive anyway, and he doesn't have a driving licence, let alone an HGV licence.

'I wouldn't worry about it Spencer. You answered a few questions, that's all, and it's only because, as they say, you have a fascination for facts and figures, and you're naïve—if you don't mind me saying so. If it came to a court case, and you were on trial, I'm sure people would speak up on your behalf. Crikey, if it came to that, I'd provide a character reference myself, and say I'd known you for years. Stop looking so worried Spencer, it won't come to that—and even if it did and you were found guilty... Spencer it's OK, honestly. I'm just saying, if it *did* come to that, you'd get off with a warning... a smack on the hand, that's all. No, not literally you giant twit.'

Spencer can't follow her at all, but when she uses words like 'trial' and 'court', he loses the power of speech, the animal's ears prick up, and if he was standing up, his legs would buckle under him.

'But listen, Spencer. I've had a thought. Because you haven't been having much luck lately, and if it's agreeable to you, I'd like to stay in your flat for a few days, see what it's like.'

'No... No Goldy... My social worker said I can't have anyone stay with me, not after what happened when Mum stayed that time. It's in my care plan. It says I might be taken advantage of and-'

'Hey, hey, hey, HEY!' She has to shout to shut him up, and he's getting more and more agitated, and rocking back and forth on the rug. 'What's all this talk about care plans and social workers? I'm not going to take advantage of you. I'm your friend, I like you and want to help you through this rough patch, because from where I'm standing, you don't have a whole lot of friends in your life. Anyway, fair's fair. You've kipped here a few nights; it's high time you repaid the favour. There's such a thing as squatters' rights you know.' Taking another chocolate, Spencer watches her unwrap it. 'It would be good for me to care for someone else. Spencer, will you stop making that face? I'm being nice to you. Isn't it nice that I'm caring?' Biting into the chocolate with her strong teeth, she tosses the foil into the embers.

'Caring, yes, caring,' Spencer says, as the wrapper flares up pink.

18

It's the next day, and Spencer and Goldy are wriggling free from the core pastilles, and not only the ones in the house, the plants and the earth; but the ones inside them, except those ones are trying to hold on fast. The wind's against them, it's a slog, their legs are like lead, and the sky's weighing down on them and it's the colour of lead. Goldy's strong, with long, powerful legs—she told him she used to swim breaststroke for the county—and once she's set her mind to something she doesn't give up.

Goldy wheels her bike, and when they're on tarmac, where it starts to rain, she gives Spencer a backie, at least until they reach the main road, where it's a dual carriageway and too dangerous, and she carries on alone, and he takes the bus.

He only has to wait three minutes, and when passing her he waves from the back seat, and she waves to him. It's as if she's pedalling backwards, when in fact it's just that the bus is going so much faster. He watches her until she's tiny, and until he can't watch her anymore on account of her disappearing round a bend.

Facing the front again, it's no good, he can't stop himself

any longer, and he thinks about bad things, and the animal paces up and down. He thinks about whether Snowdrop will like Goldy, or, after everything he's put her through, she'll be upset with him even more, hide under the bed and never come out. Mostly though, he thinks about the teenagers and how they'll react to Goldy, and perhaps they'll cut her as well, or even rape her; and he still doesn't know what it means, except it's very bad and something men do to women. The more he thinks about it, the more restless the animal becomes, baring its fangs in readiness. He can see the teenagers, or rather, feel their presence, and like the animal, they're waiting to pounce.

As the bus enters the city, and is snarled up in traffic on the approach road, he can smell the animal, or perhaps it's the teenagers, and things are muddled, and he can see the teenagers in the cage, and he doesn't like to think of them inside him.

It wasn't so bad when the bus was moving freely, and he watched the trees and hedges streaking by. Now it's constricted, they're inching along, and there's nothing to look at except vehicles on every side, leaden sky overhead and the caged teenagers inside his chest, and he wishes he hadn't said she could stay with him, but it's too late, and he's rocking and humming, and things are going to get bad, and somehow it's connected to the corpuscles.

They're all black—the corpuscles in E block—he's sure of it. If the golden pastilles flow in and out of Goldy and him when they're in the house, it makes sense that the black ones flow in and out of him when he's there, and every time he goes back to the house he takes more black ones with him. It's his fault for travelling between the two places, and now

Goldy's going to be infiltrated and become a carrier too, and he shouldn't have said she could stay.

There must have been an accident because the traffic is barely moving, and he looks over his shoulder to see if Goldy's catching up. There are teenagers in the car behind, listening to rap music, and they're restless, caged animals, looking at him in a cross way, shaking their fists, shouting things he can't hear, and maybe they want to cut him too, and he's afraid to look behind after that, and changes seats so he can't feel their eyes on the back of his head or their black corpuscles sloshing about.

It takes a long time for the traffic to get going, and still he hasn't seen Goldy, and surely she should have passed by now. Maybe she's taken a different route, or got lost. Then again, she might have crashed, and it will all be his fault again, and whatever is inside his chest seems to think so too, and wants to tear him apart. Then again, she might have changed her mind, or decided she doesn't want to care for him, and even hates him, and doesn't want to blacken her golden pastilles. He's rocking, he's humming, his head is spinning.

★

'Here, drink this.'

A black shape is making shapes with his mouth, a man, talking, and Spencer takes the plastic cup and drinks from it.

'You must have fainted. It's alright, take it easy... That's it, deep breaths. You're in the bus station. I noticed you didn't get off, and then I saw you were kind of slumped forward. Have you missed your stop?'

Spencer doesn't understand what the man's saying.

'Hello? Do you speak English? Where are you going?' He asks this slowly, over and over again.

'Spencer Frederick Morton, apartment 1919, E block, Greystones,' Spencer manages.

When the bus starts up again, and resumes its journey, Spencer can't work anything out, and it's as if it's black inside his head, and there are doors in every direction, and every one opens onto more blackness, and maybe he hasn't woken up.

Someone is holding him up and helping him off the bus, and it's like another door opening onto blackness.

'Spencer, are you OK? What happened sweetie?'

It's a lady.

'Thank you so much driver, you've been very kind. I was waiting for him. I'll take over from here.'

The lady is supporting him, and leading him to the shelter, where shapes are moving and there's a smell he knows, and she's sitting him down. Sitting beside him, she's squeezing his hand and rubbing his shoulder, and saying lots of words. And then another door opens and it's a bit lighter, and he realizes the shapes were tracksuits, and the smell was Adidas Ice Dive. And then it's bright white in his head, and he looks around, but there's no one there except for Goldy holding his hand and smiling at him.

Making their way along the path, he's wide awake now, walking normally—except for stopping every few paces and looking all around—and Goldy wheels her bike inside, and Spencer can hear it ticking. Well, she says, she's not going to leave it outside is she? Which will be another thing to petrify Snowdrop, and keep her under the bed.

Jackie from 308 is waiting for the lift with her carer.

'Hello Spencer,' she says.

'Hello Jackie, hello Mrs Smith,' Spencer says.

'Hello Spencer,' Mrs Smith days.

'Is she your carer, Spencer?' Jackie asks.

'No,' Goldy says, 'I'm his friend. My name's Goldy. Pleased to meet you.'

They shake hands, and Jackie looks her up and down as they all go in the lift.

Whenever he's in the lift with Jackie, Spencer thinks about inviting her in for coffee. He doesn't want to invite her for coffee, he's just worried he might blurt it out by accident. She'd only talk about dolls, which is what she's doing right now to Goldy, and Spencer doesn't think Goldy likes dolls either.

Convinced Snowdrop will be under the bed, when he opens the door, not only is she behind it, but shoots out into the corridor and rubs against them, and sniffs Goldy's shoes, fingers and bike. She won't leave them alone, climbs all over them when they sit down, rubs against any part she can reach, purrs like mad, and when Goldy says she's lovely, adorable and a pretty kitty, she purrs louder.

When Goldy tries the door to the balcony, and Spencer explains he's not allowed a key and it's in his care plan, she shakes her head.

There are no messages from Mum on the ansaphone, which is something.

Later, when they've both had a shower, lunch, and Spencer's shown Goldy where everything is (or rather, Spencer *and* Snowdrop, because she won't leave them alone) she says she's going to cook dinner, and they'll need to go shopping because he doesn't have a well-stocked kitchen, and frankly, he should be ashamed. She grumbles about the electric hob as well, and would have brought her camping stove if she'd known.

They go down the stairs, because Goldy says she's doing a Miss Marple on his ass, and scopes out the seventh floor landing for clues. Then, after she's taken pictures from every angle with her phone, she knocks on Mr Higgins' door, and doesn't need to ask what number because Spencer's said it so many times.

'Only too happy to help my dear,' he says on the doorstep. 'I'll run up and give you the gen.'

It's not a figure of speech either, he does run up the stairs, and he's got his tracksuit and running shoes on.

'You two need to do a bit of exercise.' He's jogging on the spot when they catch him up.

Then he goes into it, says he knows for a fact it was six a.m. when he came across Spencer, because he goes for a run every morning at that time, runs from the fifth floor to the nineteenth, then to the bottom, then all the way to the paper shop on the main road, and back up to the fifth floor again, and he's seventy-eight you know, and he's done it every single day since he retired, on Christmas Day, the lot.

Goldy says she's very impressed, and asks him to show how Spencer was lying, and Spencer gets into position, and she takes pictures from different angles, and asks Mr Higgins if there's anything else he remembers, what Spencer was wearing, and how his face looked, and things like that. He's not sure about that he says, except Spencer was fully dressed, and can he go now because his masseuse will be here soon, but it's all above board, and there's no hanky-panky.

'Well, well, well,' Goldy says when they're going down the stairs.

'What?' Spencer's trembling with anticipation.

'I'll tell you when we're outside. Walls have ears.'

Spencer's heard this one before, and he's never liked it—unless she's talking about the teenagers, how they're in the walls, and are in fact the black corpuscles.

'You were going up and not down,' she says on the path, 'and unless you sleepwalk fully dressed, I would suggest you came up in the evening, and lay there, undiscovered, until Jimmy Saville found you. You said yourself you never see anyone else on the stairs above the second floor. Then again, there could have been others who assumed you were drunk and stepped over you.'

'I've never had alcohol in my-'

'I said they might have *assumed* you were drunk you giant twit.'

The shopping trip takes hours due to Goldy despising supermarkets, and going into every foreign and specialist shop, where she sniffs vegetables, herbs and spices—many of which Spencer's never heard of—talks at length to the shopkeepers, and gets things cheap and sometimes free; and he listens to her words, and watches her face and hands.

On the way back a man holds the lift for someone Spencer can't see, but it's only Thomas.

'That's it,' he says, catching sight of Spencer behind a burka and two small children. 'It's all over. She's chucked me out.'

Covering his face with his fists, his whole body sobs, and all eyes are on him.

'I'll take 'im from now on luv,' pulling himself together, he says to Goldy.

'Excuse me?' she asks, as a jaundiced man with no cheeks gets off at the fourth floor.

'While I'm staying wiv me mum for a bit, I'll be goin' in the lift wiv 'im, just like I go in the lift wiv 'er. They're my responsibility, see.'

'Is that right,' she says, fixing him with a stare. 'I wonder what Spencer thinks about this arrangement, and whether he likes to be considered anyone's "responsibility". Spencer, what do you have to say on the matter?'

'Listen, I dunno 'oo you are luv, an' 'oo pays you to be 'ere, but 'e don't need you, 'coz as I already said,' and raising his voice, ''e's my responsibility.'

The burka draws her children closer, as does Goldy with Spencer.

'You should control your aggression,' Goldy says quietly; 'especially in an enclosed space with small children present.'

Thomas breathes deeply, his fists are clenched and his temporal artery twitches.

The burka is shouting in her language. Thomas realizes the lift has stopped and she wants to get off, and he steps outside to let them by. He's holding the doors open, breathing hard and his red eyes are rolling in his head. It's just Goldy and Spencer, and she stands in front of him. Thomas is red in the face, and seems to be trying to say something, opening his mouth several times, but nothing comes out. Something seems to pass, he exhales, relaxes his fists, steps back from the lift and is gone.

'What's *his* problem?' Goldy says, when the doors have closed and the lift jolts into action.

Spencer doesn't say anything, not when they're back in 1919, not when Snowdrop rubs against him, or Goldy tells jokes, does silly walks, and says sorry over and over again.

He looks through a book about trains, and the other two trail off to the kitchen, where Goldy plays music, and from the sounds and smells, she must be cooking. It starts off with garlic and onions, which is nice enough, and makes Spencer feel a little bit hungry, and presently there are other smells, which are exotic and fragrant, and they must be the vegetables, herbs and spices he's never heard of, and soon it's making him feel so hungry it's as if the caged animal has been lowered to his stomach, and he trails through to the kitchen himself.

'Where do you keep your kitchen knives and glasses?'

'I'm not allowed them, it's in my care plan. I can only have plastic ones.'

'Good thing I carry a penknife,' she says, raising her eyebrows.

Pulling up a stool, he watches her chop, stir, and shake her hips to the beat, and Snowdrop watches her, and Spencer watches Snowdrop watching her. He watches the steam coming out of the pots as well, and when Goldy's half-hidden behind it, he pictures her on a steam train, with shaved legs and a posh frock.

It takes so long she gives him poppadoms and three dips, all of which she's made, and he can't get enough of them, and neither can the animal.

The curry though. The curry is the tastiest food he's ever had, and the curry he learned in college is brown slop in comparison. He doesn't have the words for all the flavours, and not only the first flavours—the flavours that burst on he tongue when it's crunched and chewed. Then there's the spiciness and the way it makes his lips come to life, and makes them feel like juicy, tickly worms. Then there's the onion things she's made and the special bread, and afterwards he sits on the sofa with Snowdrop on his lap, and he can't move and the animal's sleeping like a baby.

'You told me you did some drawings of the house,' Goldy says.

He gets them, and she sits next to him and studies them one by one.

'Why did you draw all the boards?' she asks.

'What do you mean?'

'You've drawn every single board in the windows, but when I moved in there were a few missing.'

'That's how it was when I first went there.'

'That's funny.'

Spencer looks up at her.

'Not funny ha ha, funny peculiar.'

19

It's the next day and the three renegades are reclining on the carpet. For breakfast they had Eggs Benedict with Goldy's home-made bread, and she's going to bake some more with her yeast culture. She's doing all the cooking she says, because she's seen his menu on the fridge, and it's time he had some proper food.

'Your flat's a million miles away from my house- the house I'm squatting in I mean,' she says.

Spencer looks confused.

'Not literally Spencer... Or at least I don't remember arriving by spaceship. I'm talking about how everything's different. Look around you.'

Spencer doesn't know what he's supposed to be looking at, but does what he's told.

'The boxlike rooms, simple forms, muted colours, the order, cleanliness, the lack of birdsong and branches tapping at the windows, buildings in every direction, the sound of traffic...'

'Don't you like E block Goldy?'

'It's different, that's all. I can't see myself rattling about in hat big house in the winter, that's for sure. I'll be in South America by then with a bit of luck.'

'Do you mean Chile?'

'No Spencer, not Chile. Anywhere but Chile. Have you got a pair of scissors?' She's pulling at a loose thread on her jumper.

'I'm not allowed scissors, it's in my care plan.'

'Not allowed scissors? It beggars belief... Well, once again, the Swiss armed forces save the day. Where would we be without them, eh? I'd be walking about with a bobbly jumper for one thing.'

She says she's taking him shopping, and not just for food, but clothes and a new backpack, because renegades don't dress like him, and if he wants to be seen with her, and not terrorized by ruffians, he needs to dress in black and khaki like her. She says not to worry about food, she'll pay for that, because she gets her giro today; and as for the other stuff, she knows he's flush after living off hospital food for a month. So he tells her about his zero-hours contract, how he didn't get a penny for that month, and his job coach said it was the only way she could get him the job. When she puts her head in her hands, he tells her it's alright because he's got five-hundred-and-ninety-nine pounds ninety-seven in his savings account.

They go to an army surplus store Goldy knows, where she kits him out in the smallest size German moleskin shirt and combats they stock, a camouflage backpack and size six oxblood DMs, the *only* colour in her opinion, and he's more than happy to go along with her choices, because she's tough and he wants to be like her. The man serving them asks if he's a mercenary, to which Spencer turns his mouth up at the corners and Goldy fixes him with one of her stares.

They go to Greenstreet, the part of town she used to squat in, where she takes him to West Indian and Polish grocers, a wholefood shop and a fishmonger's—where she says the fish were swimming in the sea a few hours ago—and return to E block along the canal towpath, where only bottles swim, and she talks to alcoholics, and gives them money.

When they've had dinner, which is just as amazing as last night, the music's turned up loud in 1819, and when Spencer tells Goldy it's the same every other Thursday, and will go on all night, she says it'll be when they get their dole money, the same as her, and they're going on a bender like she used to. She says she's going to kick up a fuss, and goes down there, but the occupants don't hear her banging on the door, or pretend not to. They sit in the bathroom for a while, until Goldy says they can't spend all night in there, and, even with their own music they can hear the bass and feel the vibrations.

Then she has an idea, and suggests they go to his work, and see if his X-wing has turned up, and Spencer's face lights up.

'I noticed how scared you looked when we were going down in the lift and coming out the building,' she says on the train.

Saying nothing, he looks out the window at the black panorama against an inky blue sky.

'It's because of *them*, isn't it?' she says softly. 'They come out at night don't they? Don't worry.' She pats the back of his hand. 'You're safe with me. I've got my Swiss Army knife remember.'

The train trundles on through the night.

'It's like being in a castle where you live isn't it? You're quite safe inside... what with the thick, impregnable walls of your care plan... and your social worker wrapping you in cotton wool... but outside there's a moat, which is full of bloodthirsty piranhas, and the drawbridge is more like a tightrope. I feel it too. Then there's the effort of coming and going, which takes about ten minutes, what with the lift forever stopping to let people on and off, and it's infernal bleeping, and having to go through about ten doors slamming and echoing like prison doors. Who could be bothered with that day in, day out? It's dehumanising... You know, when people lived in castles, enemies were hung, drawn and quartered. Well, nowadays it's the architects of these monstrosities who should be hung, drawn and quartered. I bet the man—and it will be a man—who built Prisoner Cell Block E doesn't have to put up with one-hundred decibel gangsta rap all night, or travels up and down in a lift with complete strangers looking daggers at him, and never spent a night here. Not one single night. He probably won awards for his tower blocks, and all the wankers at the awards ceremony waxed lyrical about the purity and the stark beauty of these buildings, and then went back to their big, detached houses in leafy suburbs. Yeah, they're great, these tower blocks, great at keeping all the riff raff incarcerated and away from them.'

Steel grinds on steel.

There's someone different on the door when they walk into the supermarket. They get through a lot of security guards. Goldy says it's like going into a nightclub, and again you have to put up with a stranger looking daggers at you. Spencer is still quiet, and it's confusing to be here and not working, and passing cans of baked beans, he starts rotating them so the labels are centred; until, that is, Goldy drags him away.

Spencer knocks on the warehouse doors, which also feels odd, and then goes in because there's no answer, and Goldy stands there holding one of the swing doors open. Spencer's lost track of time and he doesn't know if it's A or B shift, but Diesel's there, and so is his stand-in, and they're both looking at their phones with their feet up.

'Well, look at what the cat dragged in. I thought you weren't coming back until next week,' Diesel says.

'I'm not working Diesel,' Spencer says. 'Have you got my X-wing please?'

'No... no I haven't.' She's noticed the backlit, yellow-outlined dungarees standing in the doorway, and gets out of her chair. 'Aren't you going to introduce me?'

'This is my friend Goldy,' he says.

'Where do you get a friend like that? Pleased to meet you.' Diesel stares up at Goldy, who's much taller than her.

'Hello,' Goldy says, shaking hands. 'Er... can I have my hand back now?'

'I'm Dimitri,' the stacker says, without looking up from his phone.

No one pays any attention.

'So, *you're* lumbered with him,' Diesel says, cocking her head in Spencer's direction.

Spencer retreats to the corner, next to the boxes of Red Bull.

'No,' Goldy says, slowly and deliberately, 'I'm not his carer, and I'm not being paid to look after him. Now, would you mind telling us what's happened to his *Star Wars* model?'

'I don't know anything about it. Maybe it's been sold. You'll have to take it up with eBay... either them or the police.'

'What's happened to... What was his name again Spencer?'

'Gordon Briggs,' Diesel says. 'He's been sacked, that's all I know.'

Motionless, Goldy considers Diesel through narrowed eyes, and Diesel looks down at the floor.

'Shall we go Spencer?' she says.

Striding away, Goldy pushes a door with each hand, and Spencer trots out before they close.

On the way out Goldy picks up a box of tumblers and a kitchen knife which Spencer says he'll pay for because he gets a discount.

'Well, well, well,' she says, when they're out of earshot of the security guard. 'She's not much of a liar.'

Spencer does his confused face.

'I'm sorry to say this Spencer, but I think she's bent. Or should I say crooked? Very, very shifty. I think she got the X-wing back and has either kept it or sold it.'

It's as if the doors in Spencer's head have all slammed shut simultaneously.

'Look at that place, Spencer.' She points. 'Take a long, hard look. Remember that Polish security guard? Remember Gordon Briggs? And think about her in there. Not very nice people. You've been in hospital a month, you've still got bruising on your face, and she didn't even ask how you were. These are the only people you've told me about as well. God knows what the rest are like.' Stopping under the cold glow of a streetlight, she shakes his slight shoulders.

'You're better than that Spencer. You could make something of your life. You could work on a steam train or you could… I don't know… make *Star Wars* models out of matchsticks. Anything at all.'

'But my job coach said…'

'Spencer!' She steps back from him, giving herself more space to swing her arms. 'Forget about your job coach… and forget about your care plan. You're your own person. You don't need to live by other people's rules.'

Striding away, he has to half-run to keep up with her, stepping in and out of pools of artificial light, and it's very quiet, except for the whooshing traffic on the motorway.

'This social worker of yours. He's got a lot of explaining to do.'

'You'd like Robert, Goldy, honestly you would. He helped me get my job.'

'A heck of a lot of explaining.'

'But he's nice Goldy, he won't rape you.'

Stopping in her tracks, and doubling over, she laughs long and hard. Spencer stands there, with his confused face.

20

It's the next day. They ended up sleeping in the bathroom—Goldy and Snowdrop on the floor, and Spencer in the bath—and then, when it got light, and the music stopped, they went to their beds, or in Goldy's case, the sofa, and slept until twelve-hundred hours.

'You only need to check you've got your keys once Spencer,' Goldy says, when they're leaving.

In a rare moment of sobriety, Mr Macready is coming out of 1911, and they say their hellos.

'We couldn't borrow your balcony key could we?' Goldy asks him. 'Just to see if it fits. I'm staying for a few days and Spencer's lost his.'

Spencer starts to say something—until Goldy digs him in the ribs.

'Of course you can. I'll go and fetch it.'

Mr Macready follows them until Goldy says it's a mess in there, please wait there a moment, and shuts the door. The key fits their balcony door, and she tells Spencer she's locked it again.

'Are you sure it's locked shut?'

'Yes, Spencer.'

'Locked tight?'

He tries to check, but she bars him.

'Look.' She tries to slide it open, and pulls with all her might. 'Happy now?' Bustling him outside, she asks Mr Macready's if they can borrow his key to get a copy made, and corrals the two of them down the corridor.

As they're walking past 1918 Mrs Jenkins and her son come out, and Thomas gives them a dirty look.

When they get to the lifts Mr Macready says he's forgotten his bus pass and goes back, leaving the others standing there, and Spencer checks he's got his bus pass again, and they all talk about the music from 1819 or rather three of them, because Thomas doesn't say a word. When the lift arrives, and Mrs Jenkins is about to step inside, he takes her arm.

'We'll wait for the next one fank you,' he says, without looking at anyone.

'Don't be so silly. We can all go down together.'

'No Mum,' he says firmly, 'we're waitin'.'

Goldy and Spencer go in sheepishly, and there's an awkward silence while three of them raise their eyebrows at each other, and the other one still won't meet anyone's gaze, and after an eternity the doors trundle along their tracks, and rattle shut, and, grudgingly, the lift jolts down the shaft.

Goldy's talking about Thomas, not that Spencer's listening, as he's watching the numbers light up in turn, and preparing himself for the lift shuddering to a halt, and someone getting on, as he always does. Not that he's got any power over it, and not that he can run. He likes to be prepared all the same, and so does the animal, pacing up and down in its own restricted space.

But it doesn't stop. The lift goes down, down, down, and he numbers have almost all lit up and gone dark again, and maybe, just maybe, they'll be alright this time. Seven's lit up... six... five... and they're nearly home and dry. Four... three... No, it doesn't. Three hasn't lit up at all, it's still at four, and if only he hadn't got ahead of himself, it would be at two by now, one, zero, and they'd be out the doors, down the path and on the main road, and it would all be over.

Goldy's banging on about Thomas when the doors judder apart, and the animal's throwing itself every which way, and Spencer's hiding behind Goldy, and he can't even look. No one gets in though, and they must have changed their mind, or perhaps they couldn't be bothered to wait any longer and went down the stairs instead, and the animal takes a breather.

Until, that is, the animal picks up the scent of Adidas Ice Dive, and goes berserk.

Goldy's still ranting about Thomas, and hasn't noticed a shape slide into the corner over her shoulder. She's not even looking at Spencer, but she notices the enlarged whites of his eyes out of the corners of her own, and that stops her in her tracks, and she knows what's happened and who it is just like that. Without thinking, she turns— and he's looking at his phone, and facing the other way—and before he knows what's happening, Goldy's brought him down and she's sitting on top of him with her knees on his arms.

'It's him isn't it?' she's shrieking. 'It's the ringleader, the one with freckles.'

The teenager doesn't make a sound beyond grunts and groans, and heavy breathing, and his body writhing on the metal floor with chevrons on it, and his new trainers squeaking—except they're getting scuffed because the lift sees a lot of traffic, and it's only mopped once a month.

Spencer wishes this wasn't happening, and now they've arrived at zero and the doors open, and there are people standing there staring.

'How could you?' Goldy bawls, shaking him by the scruff of the neck. 'How could you behave like that towards someone defenceless and weak, who hasn't done anything to you.'

She goes on like this, and she's still shouting, and her face is purple, and so is the teenager's in trying to free himself, except she's pinned him down and all his attempts are in vain.

Spencer wishes somebody would do something, but all they do is stand there and stare, and there's nothing he can do, because Goldy and the teenager are blocking the exit, and anyway, he's rooted to the spot himself, rooted by fear, and he's wet himself. If only there was a bit of space either side of them, and then he could run out, and away, and find somewhere to hide. But what about Goldy? She'd still be here, and the teenager might get up, or his friends or accomplices, or whatever they are, might turn up, and the tables would turn and they might stab her to death with or without meaning to.

Still she's screaming at him, still he's trying to break free, and still the people stand there and do nothing except stare, and there are more of them now, a big crowd has built up. His baseball cap falls off and everyone looks at it. They look at his phone too, or at least when it lights up, and which he manages to hold onto the whole time. The other thing is the beeping of the lift, which keeps starting up again and again, because the doors want to close, but they can't when there's a pair of legs sticking into the lobby, and the lift's impatient to get going again and wishes all the people would do something as well.

'Call security, call the police, do something you idiots!' Goldy's shouting things like this, and doesn't want to let him go, not after she's worked so hard to keep him there.

'Ryan!' someone is shouting, someone out of view, over and over again. 'Let me fru for fuck's sake. It's me mate. He fuckin' needs me.'

Spencer wishes he hadn't let Goldy stay with him, and he's trying to hide his wet patch, and the teenagers will laugh at him, and then stick their knives in him just the same, and the people will stand there and stare.

Hearing the other teenager, the one with the freckles redoubles his efforts, and perhaps afraid he will free himself, Goldy punches him in the side again and again, and still no one does anything or says anything, and while he's writhing in pain, she's able to haul his legs in and manages to reach the 'doors close' button, jabs at it frantically until the doors come together, squashing the baseball cap in the process, and presses the highest button she can get to without lifting a buttock or knee.

Spencer breathes a smidgen easier when the lift starts up again.

'Press nineteen Spencer,' Goldy's shrieking. 'I can't reach it. Before it goes down again. Spencer! I'm not letting go. He's got a knife in his pocket, I can feel it. Press nineteen. Nineteen, Spencer, nineteen.'

He does it. Quite what this will achieve he doesn't know, apart from going up and down in the lift forever, or until he's fainted, which he hopes is very soon. He would slump down on the floor if he could, because his legs are jelly and he's shaking all over, but he'd be closer to the teenager, so he's not doing that. And Spencer can see his face: it's angry and red, scrunched up and spitting. No, he's not doing that.

'I heard about the things you did. You pulled a knife on him and threatened to scar him. How could you do a thing like that? He's never done anything to you. Not one thing. Why don't you do something useful with your life? I bet you've never done anything good in your entire, wretched existence. How do you live with yourself? You think you're such a big man don't you? There's what..? Five… six of you, and you're all bigger than him. How can that make you feel good? You're nothing, you're dirt…' She goes on like this. It's pure rage, and she's so worked up it's as if he bullied *her*, or he's someone else entirely, and her face is purple, and spit's coming out of her mouth and dripping on the side of his head, where the hair's been shaved.

He doesn't say anything. He's not making a sound, and he's given up trying to free himself, at least for the time being.

They're about to reach the nineteenth floor—Spencer's been watching each number light up in preparation—and he's worried the teenager will make a sudden movement and catch Goldy napping, and get away. Then he'll pull his knife out and the lift will end up a bloodbath.

But when they reach the top floor and the doors open— and Mrs Panggabean from 1904 is standing there—neither of them move or say a word. Mrs Panggabean doesn't say anything either, and shuffles over to the other lift. The beeping starts up, the doors close, and the lift goes back down again. This time it stops at every floor, except for the seventh, not that anyone on any of these floors gets in, or does anything except stand there and stare. They stand there staring on every single floor, until the bleeping starts and the doors close. Every single time. Over and over again. It's like a recurring dream. Spencer's too exhausted to think what will happen when they reach the ground floor again, and perhaps so are Goldy and the teenager, because neither of them say a word or move a muscle.

There must be about a hundred faces in the lobby now, fronted by the unmistakeable forms of two hi-vis vests. Still no one says anything, as Goldy gets to her feet and so does the teenager, and someone hands him his baseball cap, which he duly dusts down and puts on. They come out of the lift and the high vises lead them through the crowd, which makes way for them like a liquid, and closes again in their wake. No one says a word the whole time, although some of them film it on their phones. It's as if everyone's exhausted, even the teenager's friends or accomplices, or whatever they are.

Goldy manages to spit on him before they're separated, and it's a good shot, landing on his face, and he's smirking, and wearing it like a badge of honour.

Goldy and Spencer are put in the back of one police car, with the teenager in another.

'I would search him if I were you,' Goldy shouts. 'He's got a knife.'

From the back seat, she twists to watch them put his hands on the side of the car, spread his legs and do a full body search. They find nothing.

'Go back,' she shouts. 'He must have dropped it in the

grass. How could you have missed that? Go on, one of you go back. It's got his fingerprints on it.'

'Settle down Miss.'

Spencer's not listening. He's looking out the window at nothing in particular, lost in thought. He's gone into himself, beyond the animal, beyond everything.

He doesn't hear anything that's being said at the police station either, while they're waiting to be attended to, because, as the desk sergeant says to Goldy, they've got a bit of a rush on. There's one man who's drunk and shouting obscenities, something about a woman who's got his children, and she hasn't got a leg to stand on. It's quite difficult to make him out though. Then there's another man who's shouting in a foreign language and is clearly very distressed. All of this makes Spencer go deeper inside himself, and he doesn't notice the teenager staring at him throughout.

Goldy's not able to help Spencer much either, although she gives his hand a squeeze a few times, and when noticing his wet patch, she asks at the desk if they've got any spare clothes, and he changes into a pair of tracksuit bottoms that are far too big. Goldy's a bit riled herself just now. She told Spencer before how she doesn't think much of the police, not after all the run-ins she's had with them over the years on demos of various kinds, and chaining herself to bulldozers, or laying in front of bulldozers during road protests. She sees them as fascists and bullies, and very similar to the teenagers, just better organised and with more weapons.

When they go up to the desk, and answer all the questions, and hand over their belongings, Goldy does the talking for both of them, and says she's his carer, and no one questions it. When they ask for her address she gives her parents'.

'Citizen's arrest, that's what I was doing,' Goldy says four times, as well as: 'Have you got that down?' and: 'I know my rights.' Mostly though, she wants the desk sergeant to know the teenager had a knife, it will have his fingerprints, and he used it to threaten Spencer.

'Thank you, Miss,' he says. 'But if you'll leave the policing to the constabulary thank you very much, and if these sorts of things concern you so much, the Force would welcome your application.'

'There's no need for sarcasm,' Goldy says. 'I want to see you write down that I felt a knife in his pocket.'

'Are you sure you didn't imagine it was a knife Miss?' one of the officers who attended the scene says.

Goldy turns on him. 'Well, I don't think he was pleased to see me, if that's what you mean. I hardly think I'm his type.'

Spencer's not listening; he's gone so deep inside himself he's almost come out the other side, and barely notices when they put him in a cell on his own, where he sits on the bed, and rocks back and forth, humming to himself. He's thinking about the core pastilles—in fact not so much thinking as picturing them. He's picturing how the black ones from the teenager have infiltrated him and Goldy, and perhaps that's why she's in such a bad mood. He wonders if there's room for all the black ones piling in on top of the gold ones, or whether the gold ones will go black. It could be like Othello, that board game he used to play in Sunrise against Raymond Patterson. He always thought he was going to win this time, but Raymond would put his last few black counters in the corners, and all Spencer's white counters would be turned over—turned black—and Raymond rubbed his hands, and Spencer had lost again.

The other thing is, now he's in prison, and will probably stay there for a long time, Snowdrop will be left on her own once more, and will either starve to death, or never forgive him. Although again, he can't think about it, and can only picture her eyes: cross, frightened and under the bed.

21

It's the same day and they're back in 1919. Goldy's on the swing seat on the balcony in a cloud of cigarette smoke. Although she gave up smoking when she left the previous squat, she's so worked up, she caved and bought twenty Silk Cut on the way back from the police station. It's alright here she tells him, but she mustn't smoke at the house because that will set a precedent, and she's going to add 'no fags' to her sign on the front door. She cleaned up the bird poo, wiped down the seats and table, and put sunflower oil on the swing seat to stop it squeaking.

Goldy's mad because they let the one with the freckles go as well, and he's probably back in the building and will think he's untouchable, can do what he likes, and will want to get even. Not that she's worried about a teenager herself, or even a gang of them, not when there's other people about at least, but she's worried for Spencer, because he can't look after himself.

Spencer doesn't want to go out on the balcony because he's not allowed to, it's in his care plan, and Robert might find out. He's sitting on the sofa with the *Golden Treasury* open on his lap, and he's turning the pages, but not reading

181

the words or looking at the pictures. Mostly he's thinking about the black corpuscles, and trying to work out where they are in his body, if they're just in the extremities or mixed in, how many there are and how many gold ones are left. It's quite nice to think about them—even the black ones—and it's better than thinking about a lot of things.

Snowdrop's keeping him company, washing herself beside him as if there isn't a worry in the world. She's been out on the balcony, but isn't keen on the swing seat.

He can see Goldy through the glass door, and looks up at her occasionally. It's nice having her here, although not as nice as being in the house with her. She doesn't fit in here, she wants to change things, and keeps saying how, compared to the countryside, everything's shit in the city; and he agrees, but he doesn't want to think about these things right now. She's lost Mr Macready's key as well, and it must have fallen out during the scuffle, or they didn't give it back to her at the police station. Spencer doesn't understand how she managed to open the balcony door, because she showed him it was locked when they left. He doesn't want to think about that either—or how Robert might find out—along with all the other things he's trying not to think about.

It's as if thinking about Robert causes Robert to think about him, and he sends a text saying he's just found out what happened and he's on his way, and Spencer's surprised because it's the evening and Robert's always saying he only works nine to five. He tries to concentrate on the core pastilles and pictures them turning over in lines like in Othello, at least until Robert arrives. He can't though, he just can't, and the animal's sharpening its claws in readiness.

Goldy stubs out her cigarette straight away, and comes

through, and there must still be plenty of golden pastilles left inside them, and they can communicate with each other. Spencer shows her the text, thinking she'll go out, or at least hide in the bedroom, but she says she wants to meet this Robert, has a few things to say to him. Spencer's powerless to do anything, and, anyway, he needs to take up his position at the window, and watch out for the mustard Fiat five-hundred—but not until Goldy's brought in her cigarettes and a mug that's sitting out there, and put the chairs back under the table, and pulled the balcony door tightly shut. It's only then that he remembers the knife and the tumblers, and hides them under the bed.

'Promise me one thing, Spencer,' Goldy says, when he's in the living room again. 'Don't mention the house where I've been squatting, because that might get back to the cops, and then it'll be no more squatting for Goldy, and no more visiting for Spencer.'

He doesn't really understand, but promises anyway, and she goes on to say he's not to mention where she lives, just don't bring it up, and, as far as he's aware she lives with her parents, but he's never been there and doesn't know where it is.

'And who might this be?' Robert asks, upon entering the living room.

'Who might this be?' she echoes. 'Is that any way to speak to anyone? And who might you be yourself?'

'Going to be like that is it?' he says, taking a seat.

'Did we say you could sit down?' Hands on hips, she fixes him with a stare.

He stands up again. 'May I sit down Spencer?'

Wide-eyed and nodding, Spencer's never heard the like.

'Thank you.' He sits back down. 'Now why don't we *all* sit down and talk about this situation that we find ourselves in, calmly, like adults, and then we can get this over with and all get back to our Friday evenings.'

Goldy folds her arms and makes a snorting sound. Hovering by the doorway, Spencer doesn't sit down either. What about the tea and protocol biscuits?

'Well, I'll just get on with it then,' and he takes some papers out of his shoulder-bag. 'This is the report the police gave me. That other community police officer phoned me... What's her name?... Anyway, it's not important.' He goes into it (during which Goldy perches on the sofa arm and Spencer sits next to Snowdrop again) and reads the investigating officer's statement, detailing everything that happened, and how the police had nothing to keep them in the station, sent them home with a warning, and told them to keep the peace. The whole time, without wanting to, Spencer pictures the one with the freckles on the floor of the lift, and his face, seething, spitting and scrunched up like a scrunched-up ball of paper.

'Well, what have you got to say for yourself Spencer?' he asks.

'It wasn't anything to do with him,' Goldy says.

'I was asking him,' Robert says. 'Well, Spencer?'

Spencer watches Snowdrop's tummy going up and down.

'Look,' Goldy says, 'I was the one who carried out the citizen's arrest. He'd told me all about these teenagers, how they'd pulled a knife on him and were making his life a misery. I knew that one of them had come into the lift by the look on his face. I'm his friend you see, and I did it for him.'

'And how did you meet this... this lady Spencer?'

'Don't "lady" me, I'm a woman.'

Robert takes his glasses off and rubs his eyes.

'How did you meet her Spencer?'

Spencer's watching his tummy, which is going up and down at the same speed as Snowdrop's, and he's wondering if perhaps, rather than the black corpuscles infiltrating him and Goldy, the gold ones have sneaked into 1919, and formed a stronghold.

'It's none of your business,' Goldy says under her breath, after a pause.

'Where does your friend live?'

'That's none of your business either.'

'Spencer?'

Spencer's found he can control the animal's breathing and heartbeat, and its tummy is going up and down at the same speed as his and Snowdrop's.

'Listen Spencer. I've been having conversations with the Manager of Sunrise and-'

Spencer loses control of the animal.

'You're a nasty piece of work, do you know that?' Goldy says, jumping up. 'You're like Nurse Ratched in *One Flew Over the Cuckoo's Nest*- In fact, you're just the same as the teenagers and the police—a bully.'

Distressed by the raised voices, Snowdrop flees, and Spencer can't keep control of his own breathing anymore, and he's wondering if he'd be able to pull the balcony door open and climb over the railings before they could stop him.

'Listen,' Robert says, standing up as well, taking his glasses off and pointing them at Goldy, as if they're a knife, 'I don't know what your game is and why you're interested in him, but I don't feel you're in his best interests.'

'I don't know where she lives and I've never been there,' Spencer shouts, remaining seated, his eyes darting from side to side.

'You're not even in your own best interests,' Goldy mutters, shaking her head. 'But tell me this: why didn't you feed his cat while he was in hospital like you said you would? She nearly died because of you.'

'Not that it's any of your business, but I delegated a junior member of my team to that particular task. She fed the cat for most of the time. However, she went on long-term sick leave a few days before Spencer came home, and failed to let me know.'

'You can't even say sorry, can you?'

Spencer's rocking and quoting train statistics.

'I've got nothing more to say to you, except that I can instruct the Court to place an injunction on you. I'm *his* social worker, not yours.' Putting his glasses back on, he bends down and stuffs the papers in the shoulder-bag.

'Thank God you're not. You shouldn't be his either. You don't do any good for him. All you're doing is exercising some need within yourself for controlling others. You tell him he can live independently, but you shove him on the top floor of this dump, full of society's outcasts, and you take away his rights. How's he supposed to live independently without knives, scissors, glasses, matches... and God knows what else?'

'Have you quite finished?'

'*And* with you breathing down his neck and telling him what he can and can't do?'

'I'll be in touch Spencer. So will Mrs Adeoye—but I don't think she's going to be very happy about this, do you?

Meanwhile you might want to give some careful consideration to the company you keep.'

Spencer's still reeling off stats and not listening.

'As for his job,' she shouts after him, as he's going out the door, 'he's little more than a glorified slave. Where's his stimulation, his self-worth?'

The door slams.

'His personal development?... Come on Spencer,' she says. 'Forget about the Flying Scotsman for once can't you? Start packing. We're leaving first thing. From now on, you're a squatter like me.'

22

It's the next day, and Goldy's not only ready, she's raring. Spencer's not ready, and he doesn't like to be rushed, but Goldy says he'll just have to put up with it won't he because they're not staying here one second longer than necessary. Spencer doesn't want to go at all in fact, except seeing as Goldy's made her mind up, he's keeping quiet. Snowdrop doesn't want to go either and she's doing sad meowing from inside the panniers, where Goldy's put her, and tied a bungee round her legs to stop her escaping. Goldy's put a few of Spencer's things in her panniers as well, and he's carrying as much as he can fit in his orange rucksack and camouflage backpack, which he's going to take on the bus and walk with for the last bit. Goldy says he can always come back for more things if need be. She packs some kitchen equipment as well, and is about to take the knife she chose for him, until deciding not to in case the police stop and search them.

She keeps saying 'come on' from the doorway, where she's holding her bike and wheeling it backwards and forwards—and Snowdrop's doing sad meows—and every time he tries to speak she interrupts him. He just has to accept it, she says, and she knows what's best for the pair of them. She says he's a squatter and an enemy of like her now (and can only take dark clothes with him). Spencer isn't entirely sure what these things mean, or even if he wants to be them. He hopes she doesn't mean he's an enemy of the *United* States, a country he's wanted to go to for years, on account of their splendid trains and buses.

On the way to the lift Spencer's legs keep buckling under him as if there's no bones in them, and, upon arrival, it's like there's a force field preventing his entry.

'Don't worry,' Goldy says, wheeling inside a few inches to keep the doors open. 'Crouch down in the corner and use your rucksacks as a shield. I'll be in front of you and the bike will act as my shield, and I'll have my Swiss Army knife open at the ready.'

Spencer can't seem to move his feet and he's shaking all over. It's as if the one with the freckles is still in there, seething and spitting, face-down on the floor.

'It's like that scene in the first *Star Wars* film,' she says, smiling. 'Han Solo is about to swing across that great big drop with Princess Leia, and all the Stormtroopers are shooting at them, and she gives him a kiss.'

She kisses him on the cheek then, distracting him long enough for her to pivot him in with the bike and trap him in there.

'You mean *Star Wars Episode IV: A New Hope*. It was Luke Skywalker, not Han Solo.'

'Whatever. I'll take either; I'm easily pleased. When the lift stops I'll let more people on, because they'll act as an extra layer of security, and if anyone's stabbed, it will be them.'

Spencer is hidden behind the rucksacks and his eyes are tightly shut.

Two people do get in early on, and, although the lift stops frequently—including the fourth floor—there isn't much space, and everyone else says they'll wait for the next one. Apart from one woman, that is, who says the lifts aren't for bikes, and there are bike racks in the car park.

'What, and have my prized possession nicked by a pikey like you?'

The doors close before the woman's thought of anything to come back with.

When they reach the ground floor, Spencer sticks close to the wall with the rucksack on his back and the backpack on his front, and Goldy on the outside, and then the bike, and that way he's protected on all sides. They make it outside, along the path, and onto the main road. Goldy says he'll be safe from here, but waits with him for the bus anyway, just to be on the safe side. Bystanders look at them when Snowdrop does a sad meow, and Goldy says it's her ringtone, and checks her phone every time.

'I forgot to bring any cat food,' Spencer says, wide-eyed, when the number 37 arrives.

'I think you just want to go up in the lift for another kiss,' Goldy says.

'But Snowdrop will starve to death.'

'Don't panic! I'll pick some up on the way.'

'Felix Doubly Delicious,' he says as he gets on the bus, and shows his travel pass to the driver, who doesn't look, closes the doors and sets the vehicle in motion, 'Ocean Feasts in Jelly,' he shouts, turning his head sideways to be heard through the crack of an open window. 'She doesn't like Meaty Selection.'

Goldy gives him the thumbs-up as she puts her earphones in.

'Mine's the same,' an old woman says, drawing on a joint for all she's worth, while Goldy wheels her bike onto the road. 'Turns his nose up at anything else, and muggins here has to make a special trip for his Lordship.'

'Give us a toke, grandma,' Goldy says, taking the proffered item, and floating down the road without returning it.

★

She's still floating when catching up with an orange rucksack and a pair of legs about to march through the gateway. She tells Spencer Snowdrop's been miaowing non-stop—not that she heard with her music as loud as it will go. Spencer doesn't hear either. He's far too preoccupied for such things, what with worrying about how Robert will react when finding out he's left E block. Mostly he's worrying about whether he'll have to go back to Sunrise, but he's also worrying about whether he'll still be allowed to do his job, go to Goldy's house or travel independently. Then there's Snowdrop. She might not like the house, might hide under a bed or run away and never come back. Every now and then, when walking along the yellow road, he stopped suddenly, as a new dilemma came to him; but he carried on every time, knowing that if he turned back he'd let Goldy down.

Midsummer has been another recent visitor to march through the cleft in the hedge and leave her calling card, as June rolls into July. Clover abounds at the track's margins, attended by so many bees they lend a heat haze to the middle distance, while grasshoppers chirrup merrily from a thousand enclaves. Aaron's Rod basks in the sun further up the bank, and higher still, the miniature clouds of umbellifers echo the mackerel sky. Eddies of wind breathe silver rivulets in the golden corn, blades of grass flutter excitedly; and the pondlets, past which two galumphing giants create their own airstreams, are feverish with activity.

Delighting in the heady feast unfolding before their eyes, Goldy's and Spencer's thought processes are diverted and lifted all the way to the curtseying poplars and round the corner. It's as if the turning off the road, leading to the white house, is celebrating their return, welcoming the two adventurers back into its bosom once more. Have both their trajectories finally been set on the right course? A new chapter? And, who knows, even Snowdrop's sad life might turn around.

Be that as it may, when they see a tiny, lime green Toblerone pitched in the garden, their synapses light up, and hearts skip a beat in unison.

Still a good way off, Goldy nestles her bike in the marsh grass—setting off a fresh volley of pleas from within—and, lowering her body, circles like a nervous dog. Beyond the house she stops abruptly, giving Spencer further palpitations, and wondering if she's seen a corpse, which seems unlikely when Goldy barks at the occupant to come out.

He can't take the suspense, and edging closer with the bike, the animal within somersaults when he sees the tent quiver like milk. The zip comes down and Goldy stays put, hands on hips, sleeves rolled up, waiting. A curly head is followed by ox-like shoulders, and there's more and more, et more, and how can there be so much, and still more comes out, and when the feet are out and the occupant's standing up on its bare feet, there's even more, and how did all that fit in there?

Goldy's still shouting, and the occupant's shouting back, and both of them shake their fists with rage. Spencer's never been in a situation like this, he doesn't know what to do, except stand there shivering with fright, and both the bike and Snowdrop shiver too.

Now they're fighting and Spencer feels faint.

Now they're embracing, laughing, and it's all been a game.

'I knew it was you when I came round the back and saw the A with the circle round it,' Goldy says.

'I shouldn't have painted it when the tent was up,' he says.

'No, I think the drips add drama and immediacy, a call to arms. Spencer, this is my little brother Ed. Ed, this is Spencer.'

Little brother? Does that mean she has a bigger brother than that? And why does he have the letter A on his tent when his name begins with E?

'Hello, Spencer,' he says.

Snowdrop meows.

'Was that you? Are you a cat?'

Spencer doesn't say anything, mainly because his mouth isn't working. Goldy's little brother is standing next to him, and not only is there more of him, he has tattoos, metal bits in his face and missing teeth, and makes Spencer more uncomfortable than Maciek did; a lot more.

'I can tell by your face I look a sight. I was asleep.'

'Asleep?' Goldy says. 'It must be six or seven. What's the time Spencer?'

'Six forty-two and nineteen… twenty…' Spencer's mouth is working after all.

'He's got a special watch. It's synchronised to Father Time's hourglass.'

'Actually it's synchronized to the nearest atomic clock and accurate to within 0.00001 of a second.'

'Spencer's a literalist.' Goldy raises her eyebrows.

Snowdrop meows again.

'A literalist talking cat. You don't meet one of those every day,' Ed says.

'No, there's a cat in here and her name's Snowdrop,' Spencer says.

'What a disappointment. I thought *you* were a cat.'

'No, I'm a human being.'

'My brother's a humourist,' Goldy says, giving him a withering look.

Presently, they troop inside and through to the living room, where, unclipping a pannier, Goldy hands it to Spencer, who, feeling petrified for Snowdrop, undoes the straps and unties the bungee. The other two are hunkered down as well, and they all watch the blue eyes blink and flit about. When she springs onto the carpet, unsteady at first, and then darts out the room, they all flinch, and Spencer goes after her.

'Leave her, Spencer,' Goldy shouts. 'She needs to investigate her environment—make sure it's safe—and all the doors and windows are closed, so she can't escape.'

When Goldy's made coffee, Ed's carried out his own investigation, and Spencer's rocked and hummed to calm himself down, they sit on the carpet, and Spencer opens a can of coke.

'Haven't you got anything stronger?' Ed asks.

'Didn't you see the sign on the door?' Goldy says.

'Yes, but I'm ignoring it.'

'You are not. You can drink and shoot up to your heart's content in your tent, but not in here.'

'What's the story behind this house do you think? It's as if the previous owner had to leave suddenly and never sold up. There are motheaten clothes in the wardrobes.'

'No, we think they were murdered, don't we Spencer?'

Spencer doesn't say anything. He's got enough on his plate, and has resumed rocking.

'Yes, I think the body is here somewhere, or buried in the garden, and it's like Cluedo, and you have to find the murder weapon and the motive.'

'How am I supposed to sleep tonight?' Ed says. 'What If it was Miss Goldy with the lead pipe, eh? Eh?' he says to Spencer, nudging him in the ribs.

Spencer's focusing on his plate right now.

'But that doesn't explain why it's boarded-up...' Ed continues. 'You can tell it's been empty for a long time—years... decades. I was in Chernobyl and the houses there didn't look as decomposed as this.'

'Ah, but it depends on the climate. It's probably damper here.'

Snowdrop sashays in, and without so much as acknowledging their presence, jumps up on an armchair and proceeds to lick her privates.

'Well, well, well,' Goldy says. 'Someone's pretty chilled—and after all that meowing!'

'She's preparing herself for a bit of rough by the look of it,' Ed says. 'Can probably smell a tom-cat. Has she been spayed?'

Silence.

'Spencerworld, do you copy, over? He's asking if Snowdrop can have babies?'

'I don't know the answer Goldy. No one's asked me about cat babies before.' He's not fully paying attention. He's far too busy watching Snowdrop and wondering what's come over her. She's a different cat.

'She's spent all her life in a tower block. Can you imagine?' Goldy says to her brother. 'Anyway, I'll make some dinner before it gets dark. Spencer, you can light the fire and candles- Spencer, I asked you to do it OK? I trust you not to burn yourself. Tomorrow we'll write up a new care plan for you, in which it will say you *can* do things, rather than you can't.'

'I'll come and help you with the dinner after I've wound up the grandfather clock,' Ed says.

But he can't find the key.

Later, when the four of them are digesting Goldy's haute cuisine and Felix's finest, and formed a semi-circle around the fire, Ed produces a small book, although a phone book would look small in his hands.

'Mum said you wanted this.'

'Ah yes, *Rumpelstiltskin.*'

She turns the pages of the Ladybird and hands it to Spencer, who stops scratching Snowdrop under the chin.

'I think you'll find I was right,' she says, her eyes gleaming orange in the firelight.

Moving closer to the fire, there's enough light to see the

page clearly. The miller's daughter's hair is brown, dark brown even, and there, behind her, a golden mountain of straw.

Later still, when he's tucked up on the sofa with Snowdrop snuggled at his side, Goldy's gone upstairs and Ed's in his tent—which must be like the Tardis—he thinks about the house, and how it's not only teaching *him* new things, but a cat as well, and has given her a new lease of life. He drifts back to the kiss that Goldy gave him in the lift. So, that's what a kiss feels like. He wonders if moving here was a good idea after all, but before he can wonder for very long, he floats away and sleeps the sleep of kings.

23

It's the next day and Spencer's worrying about things even more than he did yesterday. Yesterday was like a normal day in a way; he was just going to Goldy's house and he's done that six times before, and three of those times he stayed the night. But today is different to those three other times, because he's not going back to 1919, and Goldy has reminded him twice that this is his new 1919, and he doesn't even need to pay any rent, just put some money in a kitty for food, candles and a few other things, and do his share of chores, like washing the dishes and digging holes for latrines. He keeps thinking he has to go back to E block to feed Snowdrop, until he remembers she's here, and very happy to be here it seems. She's been dashing about, fighting with imaginary mice, and caught and killed a real mouse—her first kill as far as he knows.

His main worry at the moment is he has to go to work again tonight, which is worrying enough on its own, but not nearly as worrying as the travel involved. He's been poring over his number 37 timetable to work out which bus he needs to catch to be on time for his regular train. The problem is, all the 37s at that time of day terminate at he bus station, and he needs to approximate the times of trains from another station. Spencer is all about precision, not approximation; he's uncomfortable with approximation, which is why he likes timetables so much. On top of this, as if this isn't bad enough, there's the additional approximation of how long the three-mile walk to the bus stop will take. Goldy says she can give him a backie again, entailing another approximation—and what if she crashes or breaks down? No, there's too many unknowns in that scenario, and he said no thank you very much. Admittedly a backie would save time, and as it stands, to be on the safe side, in order to be at work by nineteen-hundred hours, he needs to leave at 15.33.

Goldy says he shouldn't ever go back there, but if he wants to spend three-and-a-half hours travelling each way and working twelve hours, on a minimum wage, zero-hours contract, where his human rights are violated, he's supporting a multinational only interested in the rich getting richer and the poor getting poorer, exploiting the third world, encouraging consumerism, increasing waste and CO_2 emissions, that's his lookout.

Ed says, whilst agreeing with his sister one hundred per cent, if Spencer accidentally picks up a bottle of vodka and a packet of fags, it would be a small victory for the little man.

Spencer's still got more than enough on his plate without piling it up higher, although he does wonder who this little man is.

He's not to worry about Snowdrop, Goldy tells him; both Ed and her are cat-lovers, they will feed her and make sure she doesn't escape, and Ed's boarded-up the cat-flap for the time being. So she knows this is her new home, Goldy thinks it's best if she's kept inside for a few days, and has filled a baking tray with earth for her.

Spencer got up at nine-hundred hours. He tried to stay in bed until twelve-hundred hours, as he usually does on the day before his first shift, but he had already been lying there worrying for an hour, so he thought he might as well get up and try to keep busy. There isn't much housework to do here, that's the only thing, although he has laid all his things out, and spent as long as possible categorizing, organizing and straightening them. Then he wrote out an inventory in case anything goes missing. Then he wrote it out in alphabetical order. Then he did it again because he made three mistakes. He can't do any hoovering or ironing because there's no electricity, although he has done lots of sweeping and mopping. Goldy sent him to get more water from the stream—and more wood, which didn't take long, and he didn't want to chop it up in case he ended up in hospital again and has to stay off work even longer.

It's 12.24, he's back to worrying, but there's only so much rocking, humming, pacing and toe-wiggling he can do. So he goes outside and watches Ed fiddling with Goldy's bike.

'Is it broken?' he asks, crouching down and peering at all the parts lying on the grass.

'Isn't everything broken?' Ed says, inspecting the chain-wheel and wiping it with a rag that has no clean bits on it.

'Robert says you shouldn't answer a question with a question.'

'Why not? Particularly when the question's broken in the first place.'

Spencer goes quiet. He doesn't like this kind of talk.

'Who's Robert anyway?' Ed asks, squinting into the sunlight.

'Robert's my social worker.'

'Do you have to work at being social? Doesn't it come naturally?'

Spencer picks the grass.

'I'm taking my sister's bike apart and degreasing every part until it's as clean as a whistle. The poor old girl needs a complete overhaul.'

'But why do you put all the bits on the grass? You might lose something.'

'True, true, I might. Really, of course I should have laid down a groundsheet first.'

'Well, why didn't you?' Spencer asks, aghast at such a basic error.

'I haven't got one. I usually work on the pavement. But look.' Ed raises his arms. 'No pavements.'

'He better not lose anything,' Goldy says, who's just come outside with two mugs of coffee and a packet of fig rolls, 'or I'll beat him black and blue.'

'I'll beat you blacker and bluer.'

Spencer is alarmed, especially as he looks like the kind of person who would beat someone black and blue.

'It's alright,' Ed says, taking a mug and a fig roll with his black hands. 'It's only talk. I wouldn't hurt a fly. I'm a pacifist.' He points at the CND symbol on his wrist, which Spencer thought was a Mercedes-Benz logo gone wrong. 'Except when it comes to my sister.' He throws a spanner at her back, but it misses and disappears in the undergrowth. 'Spencer, would you be an angel and see if you can find that for me?'

Jumping to his feet, eager to please, Spencer commences sweeping his hands from side to side.

'Are you a squatter Ed?' he asks.

'Not right now, but I can squat for a little bit if you like… If squatting's your thing.'

'Ed's a fair-weather squatter,' Goldy says from the bench, where she's writing in her journal. 'He lives with Mum and Dad most of the time.'

'Ow!' shouts Spencer, who's stung himself on a hidden nettle, continuing the search with sleeves pulled over his hands.

'Only out of familial responsibility. Mum needs a lot of help since the accident, and most of the time Dad's too deeply engrossed in chaos theory to lend a hand.'

'Our father is a professor of quantum mechanics.'

'Not your run-of-the mill professor either, Professor Emeritus of Organizational Development at Cambridge no less.'

Goldy snorts. 'Is that what he's calling himself these days?'

Spencer has no idea what they're talking about, and once he finds the spanner, he might retreat into a dusty corner indoors and rock to and fro for a bit. It's not just the big words they use that bothers him, it's the things they do. Goldy says she's writing a book, and when he asked what it was about, she said it was an Oedipal tragedy set in a psychiatric institution.

Just looking at Ed makes him nervous. The tattoos are everywhere, joined up with tendrils, as if they're in control of him, like the Krinoids in *Doctor Who*, in which Tom Baker, the fourth Doctor, fought against these plant creatures that ook over people's bodies. There's all the metal bits as well, and looking at them makes him wince, as if they're in him instead, and he imagines how much it would hurt to have holes in *his* nose and lips, and he doesn't want to, but can't stop himself. He wonders if Ed has one in his willy, even though he tries not to. He doesn't want to imagine what the pain would be like to put a hole down there, but again, he can't stop thinking about it almost every time he looks at Ed, and it makes him feel faint.

The other thing about Ed is that he never says anything simple. He can't say yes or no to a question, and instead says things that are silly or Spencer doesn't understand. What he would really like, is to meet someone who doesn't say silly things, sticks to facts and figures—and likes trains and buses as much as him. Then he could have a proper conversation.

Another thing about Ed is the bicycle maintenance, which is his actual job; he goes round fixing the Macdonald's Bikes, the bike share ones, and is paid for each bike he fixes. Whilst fundamentally opposed to a market economy, he says; until the political system's overthrown, for the time being he'll put up with it. It's very simple, he goes on to say; when he runs out of tobacco he just has to fix a bike, load the details on the app, and hey presto, he has money. It's not simple to Spencer, not simple at all. Ed might as well be fixing a rocket or doing experiments in chaos theory. Bikes are a mystery to him, and he watches in awe as Ed's big, black hands put a sprocket here and a spring there.

He likes watching Ed's hands almost as much as Goldy's, but whereas her hands seem to be dancing and are never still, her brother doesn't use his for gestures at all, only to perform tasks, and when they're not required, they hang there like bunches of bananas. The other difference about their hands is that, although Goldy has tattoos on hers, she doesn't seem to have them on other parts of her body—or at least the parts he's seen—while Ed's are everywhere, except his hands.

Spencer's alarm on his watch goes off at 14.30. This is so he can start preparing for work, only there isn't much preparing to do, and it's not as if he can have a shower. He tells Ed he can't look for the spanner anymore, and mostly he spends the hour walking round in circles and checking his watch.

When the time changes from 15.29 to 15.30, Spencer marches off at a tangent.

'And he's off!' Goldy says.

'Don't forget the vodka and fags,' Ed shouts. 'Any kind, I'm not fussy. As long as they're stolen; things always taste better when they're not yours or you get them for free…'

Spencer doesn't hear any more—not that he took in the first bit—he's far too busy marching, and concentrating on marching in case he trips and sprains his ankle.

Neither does he notice how the wind picks up when rounding the corner to be released by the poplars. Hair flying out behind him, his anorak criss-crossed with rills and runnels; while, flung about like pinballs, the bees carry out their own experiments into chaos theory.

Left, right, left, right. In the sinuous, dark-green tunnel he gets himself into such a state, he imagines hands grabbing his ankles from under the hedgerows. Breaking into a trot half the time, covering the distance twice as fast as usual, not only does he make the number 37 before the one he was aiming for, but the one before that.

At 17.07 he passes another unfamiliar security guard, oes through the swing doors, informs Dave Hennessy, le B day shift supervisor, he's one hour and... fifty-one ninutes early, and asks if there's anything he can do.

'Be right with you...' Dave says, not looking up from his hone. 'Let me just finish doing this.'

Spencer shifts from foot to foot.

'There's plenty of merch to go out, the only trouble is all he trolleys are on the floor.'

A trolley bursts in, pursued by Marion.

'Any chance of knocking off early Dave? Barry's had to vork-'

'No problem darlin',' he says, 'you get off.'

'Aw thanks Dave, you're a sweetheart.' Grabbing her bag, he bustles out.

'Bull, Bud, Becks,' Dave says.

'But I'm not supposed to touch alcohol Dave.'

'Management's left. Our little secret,' he whispers, before urning back to his phone.

Spencer shifts from foot to foot, before loading the boxes onto the trolley.

While he's putting some of the bottles in the fridge near the entrance, Aggie and Jean come in.

'Had enough of the hard stuff, Spence?' Aggie says, winking at Jean.

Looking up, Spencer does his confused face.

'From what I heard, you got ten cases of single malt for your part in the robbery. Developed quite a taste for it didn't you? And that's how you ended up in the Princess Royal for a month.'

'I fell down the stairs.'

'I know,' she says, nodding, 'because you were blind drunk.'

'I don't drink alcohol, Aggie.'

'Yeah, and I'm the Queen of Sheba.'

'Leave the poor boy alone,' Jean says, reaching across Spencer for a chilled can of Red Bull.

24

It's nine days later and Spencer's in the garden at 1919a, which is what he's calling Goldy's house now, and the white house before that, to avoid confusion. The hot weather has continued unabated. Every few days there's a thunderstorm (when Spencer counts the miles between the lightning flashes and rumbles) and they all go indoors to watch the short-lived downpour from there. Goldy says it's further proof of climate change, and as England moves closer to a tropical climate, Scotland heads towards a polar one, where it will soon be dark all the time and the Scots will go blind, due to no longer needing eyes, like cavefish. Spencer doesn't know what she's got against Scottish people, and only the other day she was saying Scotland should be separate from England.

One of the reasons for calling the house 1919a is because he's decided to stay in the original 1919 when working. He was so exhausted when he came back from his first shift, having had such a long commute and working one hour and fifty-one minutes extra, he could hardly keep his eyes open when walking those last three miles. Then when he went to bed he was so worried about being disturbed, as well as

207

sleeping through his alarm, he woke up every half-hour and hardly got any sleep at all. Even though he left later for his second shift, he couldn't catch himself up, and turned into a zombie. Returning from his third shift, when he would normally get up at thirteen-hundred-hours, he turned into a log and didn't wake until late in the evening, when Goldy and Ed were about to go to bed themselves. He was so worried about never getting into any sort of routine, and being tired all the time, he came round to the idea of staying in 1919 on workdays and a on days off. Goldy said he's got two homes, his city penthouse and his country retreat, so he must be a rich Tory. Spencer said she was one too, because she can stay in 1919 anytime she likes. Not bloody likely, she said.

Another reason for commuting from 1919 is that Diesel said he smelt bad on the third shift, and he knew it was because he hadn't had a shower in four days. He nearly let slip that he was living somewhere else, and there wasn't any running water, until he remembered it was a secret.

He was worried about bumping into *them* of course, which is what he's calling the teenagers these days, making them less of a threat, like they're far away, and even when they're near they're hidden or trapped in another dimension. Not that changing their name makes *that* much difference. He still thinks they're going to get him, the wording of which is in itself another way of ignoring the inevitable and brushing it under the carpet. They're going to kill him, there's no two ways about it, and every time he pictures the one with the freckles in the lift, with his face red, angry, scrunched up and spitting, he knows it all over again.

He came back early on the day before his next shift so he could go to bed for a bit, but he was too unsettled to get under the covers, and couldn't relax without Snowdrop. So he looked out the window and thought about going on the balcony. To begin with all he could do was slide the door inch by inch, and just doing that had the animal on its feet. He tiptoed out there, because he got it into his head that Robert had set up microphones or was listening underneath through a glass. The next thing was to sit on the swing seat and swing back and forth; and then, little by little, he looked over the edge and rested his elbows on the railings, softly at first, in case it gave way, and gradually building up the pressure. He was also worried that there was a hidden camera, and Robert would storm in any moment, chloroform him and take him back to Sunrise.

Nothing happened, and he gradually relaxed. It was so much nicer to be feeling the breeze on the balcony, rather than looking at the view from behind glass.

It was then that he saw five tracksuits leave the building far below, and dashing to get his binoculars, he saw one look round, and he had freckles, and he knew it was them.

He realized then he had to leave straight away even though it was only 16.36, because they might have gone to the shop and be back any minute. He'd already had a shower and everything was ready. For the first time ever he didn't read the Going to Work List on the back of the door—which was very difficult to do, even though he knows it off by heart—and only checked his keys once. He ran to the lift, and fortunately it didn't stop, and went down so fast the animal was left behind, and then he ran out the building.

The following day he set his alarm for sixteen-hundred hours, and after a speedy shower, he took up his station again, bowl of Rice Krispies in hand. He saw them leave again at

16.37, and the third day at 16.35. This is an enormous relief and he's only getting half an hour less sleep than normal.

Goldy's told him not to say anything to anyone about the house, no matter how nice they seem. They might get information out of him the same as his whisky robbery accomplices, and it's none of their business.

He's back in 1919a, sitting outside with Goldy. She's made a construction with blankets around the bench, keeping the sun off them later in the day, when the sun's lower in the sky, and Spencer's even taken his anorak off a few times even though he feels undressed. Goldy's been wearing a bikini, and the first time she came out in it he didn't know where to look, and that was when he found out she hadn't got any tattoos on her body. She caught him looking, and he looked away. She said it was OK to look a little bit when they were having a conversation, but not when she was looking the other way because that makes a woman uncomfortable. He wondered how she knew he was looking, but, nodding vigorously, he didn't ask. She asked him if he'd ever seen a woman in a bikini before, and he thought about it long and hard, and said no, except for Mum, but she said mums don't count.

He prefers looking at her face anyway. She has so many expressions, and even when she's not talking or moving, her face keeps changing, or at least her eyes do. He can't put into words how they're changing, he just knows they are, and it's like clouds drifting across the sky. Another thing about her eyes is how sometimes they go glassy in the sunlight. That's the only way he can describe it. It's as if the pastilles—which is what he's calling the core pastilles now—have come to the surface and are looking out of her eyes, and he wishes

...e could see them under a microscope because he knows they're beautiful.

Mostly, apart from using her phone and smoking (breaking her precedent) she writes in her journal and he reads his books. Sometimes she asks him what's another word for delirious or can he think of the names for any shades of orange. He doesn't know what delirious means, and thinking of orange enamel paints for Airfix models, there's just one and it's called 'orange'. He doesn't know the answers to any of her other questions, but she keeps asking anyway. He told her if she wants to write about trains or buses he could help her lots. She said they would be the last subjects she'd want to write about. Goldy encouraged him to read one of her books, and he tried hard, very hard, but there didn't seem to be any facts. She gave him two more, and when he couldn't get beyond the first page, she said he was a lost cause.

Snowdrop's going outside now—or rather, staying outside. To start with she sniffed every inch of the doorstep, and then, when she heard rustling, she leapt into the under-growth and came out with a mouse. It didn't take long for her to go off exploring. He followed her from a distance the first time, but she kept stopping and looking back, as if she didn't want him to be there. He let her go on alone and she didn't look back once, and he felt a bit sad. Goldy says he just has to accept it; cats are loners, and it's not right when they're cooped up indoors all the time, and in her opinion people in blocks of flats shouldn't be allowed pets. She still comes back for food and sits in front of the fire on the rare occasions they have one. She comes in through the cat flap in the outer door and they leave the inner door open all the time.

Ed's been away a lot as well, and Goldy thinks he's got a girlfriend hidden away somewhere. Spencer pictures a girl in a cupboard or a trunk—or a coffin, because he looks like the type of person to have a vampire girlfriend, and perhaps, unlike her, he's a hybrid who can come out in daylight.

Ed turns up when they're both sitting on the bench, and it's like a scene from a Western because Spencer sees him wheeling his bike from a long way off, and even more so with the sun behind him. He doesn't look like someone out of a Western though, except for a modern-day one like the *Mad Max* franchise.

'Hello stranger,' Goldy says.

'Hello commoner. Can't you put something on? You'll be giving Spencer ideas, and I've had a curry.'

What ideas Spencer can't imagine, and how a curry's connected to clothes another mystery.

'It's alright for you to parade about in your undies, but I've got to be all demure have I—in this heat?'

'You couldn't be demure if you tried,' he mutters, rummaging in the big paint tin bolted above his back wheel. 'Look what I caught back in the old country, and packed in ice for the journey.' Producing two large trout, he waves them in Goldy's face.

'Haven't you got any bikes to fix?' she says, snatching the fish and standing up. 'I suppose it's my job to descale and gut them.'

'What do you think of her arse?' Ed asks, once Goldy's a safe distance.

Spencer doesn't say anything.

'Am I not supposed to ask you things like that?' Ed asks, aking a bottle of Guinness out of the paint tin. 'Just letting 'ou know I've got no problem with you looking at her arse ny time you like Spencer old chap. If you like 'em on the crawny side. Me—I prefer a bit of meat.'

When Ed sits down next to him, Spencer budges up s much as he can without toppling off. Looking up when eeing a glint, he's shocked to see a flick-knife, and immedi-tely thinks Ed's an assassin hired by *them*. This thought lasts nanosecond, when the blade is used to remove the bottle op, folded up and returned to his person. It happened so ast Spencer and the animal were too stunned to move a nuscle—are still in a state of shock and disbelief.

'Cheers.' He takes a draught.

Spencer watches his Adam's apple bobbing.

'Boy, that's good. Twenty-seven miles and still cold... I ised to open bottles with my teeth, but look where that got me.' He points to a gap.

'How did you lose your other teeth?' Spencer thinks he might regret this question.

'This one,' Ed says, working tobacco and rizlas free from his back pocket, 'this one was from a whiteout on my bike... This one was a whiteout after too many spliffs... And this one down here was a fight over a girl.'

He does regret it. He doesn't know what a whiteout is or what it means to fight over a girl. He likes watching Ed's hands though, especially when they're rolling a cigarette. His hands are so rough and dirty, and he likes that about them. Mainly though, he likes the way they move, and how they look separate from the rest of him, as if they belong to someone else, someone who says facts rather than silly things.

'Answer me this,' Ed says, lighting up, stretching his legs out and taking a drag. 'When did things stop having any meaning? I rode through a town today and happened to notice the name of a shop. It was called Quiz. But here's the thing Spencer; it's a clothes shop, and I know it is because there were mannequins in the window. And it got me thinking... Why is it called Quiz?'

Spencer knows when people talk like this and don't look at him, they're talking to themselves, but still wonders why he's getting cross about a clothes shop.

'Does it sell quizzes? Fine if it did. But no, it does not. Well, as I was riding through the rest of the town and out into the fields, I thought of all the clothes shops I could. Of course there's some that are people's names, and I don't have a problem with them. There are others with aspirational names like Mango and Monsoon, and I don't have a problem with them either. Mangos are ripe, healthy... exotic... and make you think of breasts and buttocks. Monsoons are exotic as well and make you think of places that are hot, with bright colours that you want to go on holiday to... and of course rain's refreshing and revitalizing. But Quiz? Jigsaw? Gap? These names don't make any sense at all. They're meaningless. I might as well open a clothes shop and call it Woodlouse... or... or Axle Grease, or Depression, or Spreadsheet, or...'

Relighting his roll-up and puffing like crazy, he searches the horizon. Spencer searches too.

'People from the Dark Ages –' (he turns to Spencer) 'which weren't dark ages at all –' (and back to the horizon)

would shake their sensible heads in disbelief.' (Back to
pencer) 'You should understand—you're a literalist.'

But he doesn't understand, and he wishes Ed would take
his quizzes, his woodlice and his metal bits in his face far
away, and leave Goldy and him alone.

25

It's two weeks later and Spencer's on the balcony of 1919 looking out for *them* before he goes to work. The trouble is it wasn't a Sunday the previous times he waited for them. Perhaps the place they leave for between 16.33 and 16.39 is a youth club or somewhere like that, and it's not open on Sunday. He didn't consider this possibility, and often forgets what day it is anyway, what with working three on, three off. Now that it has happened, and he's realized it's a Sunday, he's panicking; he's panicking a lot.

It's 16.51, still he hasn't seen five tracksuits come out, and the railings are clammy in his grasp. He doesn't have to leave until 17.42, but any later than that he'll miss his train and be late for work. More than other people being late, he can't bear being late himself. He finds it difficult to cope with—no, *impossible* to cope with. He doesn't want to think about it though, because even thinking about it is difficult to cope with. All he can do is hope with all his might they will come out before the time changes from 17.41 to 17.42.

The other thing troubling him is he hasn't seen or heard from Robert, not since Goldy sat on *him*, which is what he's calling the one with the freckles now, to make him seem urther away. He's trying to forget when it happened for the ame reason, although he *does* remember, he remembers all oo well, and it's not always a blessing to have a memory like his.

He sees Robert every month without fail, it's in his care plan, but now it's August and it's been six weeks. He's tried phoning eight times, and texted twice, and still he hasn't heard anything. On top of this, he hasn't heard from Mrs Adeoye either, and Robert said he would after being in the police station. Maybe they're both sick to the back teeth with him for giving them so much paperwork, they're not going to have anything more to do with him, and the next time something bad happens, he'll go to prison.

It's 17.09, he can't stand the suspense any more, and feels that if he looks over the edge of the balcony any longer, he'll have an uncontrollable urge to jump.

He's had an idea. He's going to take matters into his own hands for once in his life. He's too nervous to use the lift or stairs on his own, and he can't ask Thomas to escort him, not after Goldy said she was doing it from now on. But there is another way down, and he doesn't know why he's never thought of it before. The rubbish chute. All he has to do is wrap himself in blankets and towels, and a bin bag on the outside, and then he can go down, because the skip's emptied on Monday, and it will be a soft landing. It's at the back of the building as well, and no one hangs about there.

Taking everything he'll need with him, he locks the door as usual. There's no one in the corridor, no one in the lobby, and he wraps himself in two blankets and steps into the bin bag, which has two towels folded up at the bottom. He can pull down the handle easily and flop into the loading container. It's so simple and clever. It'll be a bit of a squeeze and he's heavier than most rubbish going down the chute, but that's the only difference, and he's even in a bin bag.

If it's so simple and clever, why doesn't he get on with it? He better get a move on, because now one of the lifts is coming up, and he's opposite them, and he can see the numbers lighting up in turn. Four, five, six... Why doesn't he get on with it? He can't seem to get into the loader, and not because of any physical problem, and not because he's scared about the landing either. No, what's stopping him is the pustules, which is what he's calling the black corpuscles now, although the word in itself makes him feel sick, but that's how it should be in a way, because the thought of them makes him feel sick. Eleven, twelve, thirteen... It's the thought of the pustules being in the building, moving as one, moving fast, and dripping out the sides of the rubbish chute. Drip, drip, drip. Not only that. If they're connected to *them*, or even *are* them, they could morph into flick-knives, flick open as he falls, and slice him to ribbons, and by the time he lands in the skip, he'll be in bits—bits of meat and blood, and the binmen will wonder why someone's thrown all this meat away, and flies will lay eggs on his corpse and maggots will devour what's left.

seventy, ding. The doors open and a burka comes out with two small children, and they don't notice him standing there inside a bin bag, because she's telling them off in her language and they might think he's another burka. Going back to 1919, he leaves the blankets, towels and bin bag in a heap.

He knows it's silly to think about things like pustules morphing into flick-knives, that this is the kind of thing that appens in sci-fi, not real life, and he would be annoyed if omeone else said it. He of all people knows this, because ıe's all about logic, facts and statistics—things that make .ense. He knows it's his imagination running away with him. Ie knows these things, but keeps thinking them just the ;ame, and once he has a thought like this, about pustules norphing into flick-knives or something, the thought has a ife of its own, he can't stop it and round it goes.

It's 17.21, he'll be late if this carries on much longer, but ıe doesn't know how to leave the building, or what to do or ınything, and both he and the animal are at their wits' end. He's walking round the lobby and going past each of the doors in turn. Past the lift doors, past the door to apartments 1901 to 1910, past the door to the stairwell and past the door to apartments 1911 to 1919. He'll have to go down the stairs; it's the only option, and he better get a move on because they take longer than the lift.

Opening the door, he wedges himself in the gap, otherwise it will swing shut. There's always a breeze in the stairwell, and it smells of disinfectant and loneliness. He can't seem to go any further, that's the thing, and he sees himself as Snowdrop, because she likes to sit in doorways. He can't go forward, not even a nanometre, and if he does he's sure to fall. Neither can he go back. Going back means not going to work, and he can't do that. He's not ill or anything, and if he doesn't go to work he won't be paid.

It's 17.29, the other lift's coming up the shaft, and still he can't move. Ding. It's Mr Macready, and he doesn't notice Spencer wedged in the doorway opposite, and, after a couple of failed attempts at opening the door, he stumbles down the corridor to 1911, luckily for him the first apartment on the left.

It's 17.31, he doesn't know what he's going to do, and feels faint, and the sweat's pouring off him, and Diesel will say he smells again, if he does make it to work that is.

It's 17.33, he hears footsteps on the stairs way below, and it's hard to tell where they are because of the echoes. The fact that they're getting louder, suggests it's someone coming up, and as they grow louder still, and the person hasn't arrived, suggests more than one; louder still, and it must be several. It's *them*, they're coming for him, it sounds like they've already got him and they're running over his head, and he's rooted to the spot, and he wets himself again.

They're coming up and they're going to stab him to death while he's standing there, but because he's wedged in the doorway and it's a fire door, he'll be trapped between the door and the frame, and his blood will flow down both sides. The police won't be able to move him, not until they've done a thorough investigation and taken evidence, and everyone in the building will be coming up to take pictures and sharing them on social media.

The animal wants to get at them—even if Spencer doesn't—leap out of his chest wall and tear them limb from limb.

But it's not them, it's not them, it's not them. It's Mr Higgins from 504 and he's running, and that's why it sounds like a herd of elephants.

'Not bad... for a... seventy-nine... -year-old,' he says, and it must have been his birthday recently.

He's red in the face and panting, on account of running up the stairs, and Spencer's panting at the thought of it—

and the animal's panting too but it was doing that already. Spencer knows he's going down again, all the way to the bottom, and then back up to the fifth floor again. This is Spencer's chance; he's going to run down the stairs with him—or rather, just behind him. He's having a rest right now and doing a few stretches, and Spencer wishes he'd get a move on because it's 17.39, and if he's not careful he'll miss his train.

'Do you mind if I run down the stairs with you, Mr Higgins?' Spencer asks.

'Not at all sonny. But you'd better look lively. I don't hang about you know.'

And he's off.

He's not that fast, Spencer has no trouble keeping up, wishes he'd go faster, and keeps checking his watch—at least on the landings. He's thinking more about being late for work than *them*, that's one good thing. When realizing this fact, he thinks about them some more; a lot more. He daren't look at the walls, and can't hear anything apart from the sounds of their feet and panting, but imagines black liquid dripping down, drip, drip, drip, and wishes Mr Higgins would speed up.

There's big numbers on each landing and he can see them without looking up. Nearly there, nearly there. On the fourth floor there's a ball of chip paper, scrunched up angry and tight.

Spencer runs out the building, swivelling round and checking every direction as he goes.

Until, that is, as he hurries round to the path, hearing a shout, he sees Mrs Jenkins.

'Coo-ee!'

'I'm late for my train,' he shouts back, clocking Thomas behind.

'I've got a letter for you.' Thrusting it in his hand, it's like a baton change. 'I just happened to notice it sticking out of your box as I was looking in mine. I was going to bring it up for you.' Or words to this effect, as he's too far away to hear properly.

He makes the train with a minute to go and he can relax, and he's got a spare uniform at work to change into, and tomorrow he's going to 1919a, and he's so relieved not to have to worry for three whole days. He knows something has to happen, something has to change, because he can't carry on like this. What though? What can change, and will it be good or will it be bad?

As the train leaves the station, E block can be observed in the gaps between buildings, and it looks black with the sun behind it, and he's never thought before how it's like the monolith in *2001: A Space Odyssey*, which he's got on Blu-ray and watched seventeen times, and while it's incomprehensible, he enjoys it nonetheless.

As the tower block disappears for the last time, it hits him right between the eyes: the three days spent in 1919 is the time of darkness and those in 1919a the time of light. In 1919, not only is he surrounded by pustules that are trying to get him, he sleeps in the daytime, works at night, and even when it's light outside at the supermarket, he doesn't know about it on account of there being no windows, except at the front. When he's at 1919a, where everything on the inside and outside is drenched in light from the golden pastilles, he's mostly in the garden in the daytime, where it's sually sunny, and at sundown they sit in the living room with candles, and sometimes light the fire.

He's bought more tea lights, and even though they weren't doing 'buy one, get one half-price' anymore, he still bought two boxes, sneaked them in, and into the pots without Goldy noticing—and she still didn't notice when all twenty-eight were lit up. She said things could never be the same again, but it's not true, because all the candle pots are shining bright again.

26

It's the next day, Spencer's left work, he's on the yellow road to the house. Wandering into the middle of the road, he's so tired he can't keep his eyes open. Meandering through the gap in the hedge, he doesn't notice the changes in the surrounding flora, concentrating instead on not tripping over the rock-hard rills, the ruts, in the overgrown track. Spring and summer growth has slowed to a gentle oozing here, a seepage there, in pockets where nothing is achieved beyond self-love, conceit and complacency. Threadbare and thinning out, the flowers, reminiscent of market stalls half an hour before shutting shop, make one last push at propagation. The grass is sickly yellow; the pondlets have all but dried up—no matter, the frogs are long gone, a few sex-addled grasshoppers lay down rusty rhythms, while most of the insects have hidden their eggs, laid down in the dirt and died. Only the wheat, swishing torridly on the horizon, is ripe with promise.

It's that eerie limbo before autumn sets in. There's nothing much to do, except pack up and wait for winter to do her worst. A handful of fruits here, a cluster of nuts there, nothing more. Even the mighty poplars are on the wane;

heir leaves half-eaten, their shine faded. Once July is done nd dusted, the life-force starts to ebb. The ants and bees ave dwindled, with the survivors paring back their oper- tions and keeping their colonies ticking over until spring.

The hapless adventurer takes nothing in. He's worn out, is life-force all but going through the motions, and if he doesn't pare back his own operations, he'll keel over beside he other casualties. All that's to be done is open the door vith the key Goldy gave him, put down a fresh bowl of ood for an absent Snowdrop, strip, climb into his sloughed bedding, and sleep.

Later, when emptying his backpack, including food for hem all and another box of Terry's All Gold Darks, he comes across the letter, which he'd forgotten about. It's one of those stern-looking envelopes, the only kind he gets, a bill or appointment too serious to email. Yawning non-stop, he ries to take in the words while putting his socks and shoes on.

Just then Goldy comes in from outside.

'Hello, Sleeping Beauty,' she says.

Holding a beat-up, blackened saucepan, her hands are stained dark red, and Spencer wonders if she's smashed Ed's head in with the saucepan.

'What's your letter? Something nice?'

As she comes closer and he hands it to her, he sees the pan contains blueberries, and his first reaction is disappoint- ment.

'Learning Disability Team, Care in the Communi- ty, North East District Social Work Department. What a mouthful. If you sent them a letter and got one of the words wrong, or in the wrong order, it probably wouldn't get there, because there will be hundreds of offices with very similar names, doing similar work—or quite possibly the exact same work.'

Spencer's not listening. He's three-quarters asleep and Goldy's wearing her bikini.

'Comic Sans! What the actual fuck… "Dear Spencer, I am writing to you…"' She reads the rest in silence while biting her lower lip.

She's still holding the saucepan, except now she's cradling it to her belly; and leaning forward, Spencer peeks at the ripe fruit.

'So that other plonker's on long-term sick leave, this plonker's taken over and he wants to… How does he phrase it?… "say hello". I'll say goodbye to him if you like.'

'Where shall I put these?' Ed shouts from the hall, and, semi-naked, strolls into the living room with a colander of blackberries, very much alive. 'The prodigal son has returned. What news from the world?'

Spencer, now standing, shifts from foot to foot.

'Look at this,' Goldy says. 'It's from his new social worker.'

'What happened to the old one? Did he become antisocial?' Ed says, scanning the few sentences. 'Long-term sick leave eh? You know I used to have this job with the Council Spencer.' Ed puts the colander down. 'Yes, I worked as a groundsman; you know, digging up flower beds in parks, stuff like that. While I was there several people went on longterm skive—I mean sick leave—for six months, and then they made a full recovery, right as rain, and came back to work. Do you know why?'

Spencer doesn't.

'Because the Council pays full wages for six months,

hat's why, and then it goes down to half. And do you know
vhat they were all sick with?... Nervous debility. Know what
hat is?... I'll tell you. It's a fancy name for stress. Quite how
i gardener can be stressed I do not know, and-'

'I bet it's stress that this one's sick with,' Goldy interrupts,
and I'd like to think I played a small part in bringing him
down.'

'Did you meet him?'

'I had that misfortune. Pedantic, patronising control
reak. Treated Spencer like shit. He's practically a prisoner
n that flat.'

Spencer isn't entirely sure what they're talking about, but
ne wishes they'd stop. He needs to go to the toilet for one
thing, except Ed's standing in the way; and for another, he
doesn't like this talk of prisons, doesn't like it one bit.

'Did you notice the font though?' Goldy asks her brother.

'Comic Sans. Get thee behind me Satan! The font that
shouts, "fun, fun, fun". It's OK on a summer fete poster, but
not a serious letter about someone's future.'

'Yeah. I wonder if... What was his name again?' Goldy
grabs the letter. 'Jed Penrose. Sounds like a *Blue Peter* pre-
senter. I wonder if he uses it for all his letters... "Dear Mrs
Jones, we are sorry to inform you your son has died of a
heroin overdose." Can you imagine?'

Ed doubles over.

'You know what?' she says. 'I reckon if the Nazis had
used Comic Sans in their propaganda leaflets we'd all be
speaking German now.'

Spencer goes out the other door—the long way round—
through the dining room and the scullery.

Later, when they've stopped talking about comic sands,

and he's helped Goldy stew the berries and put them in jars she says she's going to get some ice cream from the village shop, because she's got a craving to have it with the fruit.

'Can I come with you?' he asks.

'No, I'm going on my bike.'

'Please, Goldy.'

'I'm not giving you a backie Spencer. You'll slow me down and I want to get home before it melts. I'll get you a cold can of gutrot as well.'

He doesn't know what to do with himself when she's gone, and wishes Snowdrop didn't keep going off on her own, because it's at times like this he needs her.

Spencer finds himself standing by the window watching Ed fiddling with his fishing-rod. He's always fiddling with something. It's mid-afternoon, but still hot, and he's bare-chested, and Spencer looks at his tattoos and brown skin. It's quite hard to see him clearly, what with the sun behind him and the dirty window. Spencer continues watching him all the same, seeing as he's got nothing better to do, and anyway, he's not really watching him, because his mind's drifting. He's looking at his brown torso, his brown legs and his brown hair, and they're all flat and fuzzy, like a scrap of brown paper. The more he stares at the scrap of paper, the fuzzier it becomes; and, not only that, because now there are soft, wispy bits wafting over the surface. It's not the pastilles is it? Is that what he can see? Is he actually seeing the tubes of pastilles flowing in and out of Ed's body?

He wouldn't have thought the pastilles would go in someone with tattoos and metal bits in their face, not that he *had* thought about it. Then he notices it's not just Ed; he can see the pastilles everywhere: in the fishing-rod, in the plants,

e tent, the trees and the sky. They're in everything, and
verything's connected, and pulsing with life-force. And he
els he's seen something he wasn't supposed to, something
cret, and he feels giddy, but more than anything, he feels
od.

The stench of stale sweat brings him to his senses, and
rning back to the gloomy interior, Ed's standing there, and
jumps out of his skin.

'You look like you've seen a ghost,' Ed says.

Spencer wonders if Ed *is* a ghost.

'Anyway,' he continues, 'rather than standing in here
atching me, why don't you come outside and watch me
ose-up instead? You might like to see how a fisherman
repares his tools.'

Trailing out in his shadow, Spencer's preoccupied with
hosts, whether Ed knows Bill Poster, and could get his
-wing back.

'You've missed the boring part: fixing the reel on this
od, which had jammed. But I've saved the best bit for you.
ou're going to learn how to make flies. Me and my old man
re going salmon-fishing tomorrow, and at this time of year
ou're only allowed to fly-fish for salmon.'

The big hands twist and weave green and blue thread
nd tiny bits of pheasant feathers around a hook to make
omething resembling a damselfly. It takes a long time and
e gives Spencer a running commentary. Not that Spencer's
istening, and it doesn't seem to matter that he's not—let
lone saying anything—because Ed carries on regardless,
nd doesn't look at him. Mostly he's watching the hands, the
lackberry stains, the tiny creases, the hairs on the knuckles,
he dirt under the bitten nails, how the fingers and nails are

different shapes, and how the hands move. He thinks abou
the pastilles under the surface as well, and he wonders
some of the pastilles in him have been in Ed and some of th
ones in Ed have been in him. The more he thinks about i
the more certain he is and the more he likes the idea.

'You think the sun shines out of my sister's arse, don
you? I've seen the way you look at her,' Ed says all of
sudden.

The words are viscous in Spencer's ears and take som
moments to dribble into his brain, where a stab is made a
deciphering them, and even then he doesn't answer.

'I'm not one to give advice normally, and can't stan
anyone giving me advice, but I will just say this. Don't expec
anything from her. A flighty mare, that one. She might seen
passionate and caring, and she might say she's going to do
this, that and the next thing. But then "poof"! She's gone.

'Now, for this one, I'm going to introduce some re
cotton along with the blue and green. Just in case the other
don't catch the salmon's eye.'

Spencer's thinking about the pastilles being made o
sunshine, and imagining Ed's hands peeled back to revea
light.

'Who's up for forest fruits and ice cream?'

They'd both been so engrossed they hadn't heard Goldy'
footsteps.

'Just coming,' Ed says.

'I'm not waiting. The ice cream's half-melted as it is.'

When they've had their fill, Ed says he's got to get going
soon, but not until he's shown Spencer something else.

'This is one of Snowdrop's kills,' he says, when they've
gone round to the front of the house. 'She used to leave